Loving
wanda
beaver

Loving Wanda Beaver

Novella and Stories

by **Alison Baker**

CHRONICLE BOOKS

SAN FRANCISCO

Some of these stories have been previously published as follows:
"Loving Wanda Beaver" in *The Gettysburg Review* and in *Prize Stories 1995:
The O. Henry Awards*, "Ooh, Baby, Baby" in *ZYZZYVA*, "The Rich Man's
Easy Charm" in *The Northwest Review*, "Everything Is Nothing But A Learning
Experience" in *The Black Warrior Review*, "Convocation" in *The Alaska
Quarterly Review*, "The Third Person" in *Sonora Review*.

Printed in the United States of America.

Library of Congress Cataloging-in-Publication Data:

Baker, Alison, 1953–
      Loving Wanda Beaver : novella and stories / Alison Baker
          p. cm.
      ISBN 0-8118-1064-X
PS3552.A399L68   1995
813'.54 — dc20   95-12600
                                                  CIP

Book and cover design: Brenda Rae Eno
Composition: Suzanne Scott

Distributed in Canada by Raincoast Books,
8680 Cambie Street, Vancouver, B.C. V6P 6M9

10 9 8 7 6 5 4 3 2 1

Chronicle Books
275 Fifth Street
San Francisco, CA 94103

for
M&D.
Have arrived Nome.

Contents

Loving Wanda Beaver

Oleander Joy could not have said which she loved more, detasseling corn or Wanda Beaver. Most girls detasseled for a few summers during high school and then went on to other jobs, but Oleander kept going back. She loved easing through the cornstalks under the summer sun, sliding her hand up toward the tip of tassel after tassel and then yanking sharply so that the tassel came off intact in her palm. Watching it fall from her hand to the ground, she imagined the millions of nascent corn germs that were torn away, never to reach the silk of their own developing ears, banished so that the alien corn planted in every sixth row could fertilize the entire field unchallenged. Thousands of tassels lay unspent in the field, trampled by detasselers, drying up uselessly, to be turned under by huge heartless machines in the late summer after the mature ears of hybrid corn were harvested.

But Wanda Beaver, her crew boss, was just as much a delight. The thrill of catching a glimpse of Wanda's skinny brown barely clothed frame here and there among the cornstalks! The wave of heat that rippled through Oleander, from her face down through her body and on to her knees, when Wanda now and then bared her huge white front teeth in a smile aimed in Oleander's direction! Life in the summer was an uninterrupted anticipation of the pleasure to be felt every ten seconds in the palm of Oleander's hand, and at scattered and irregular times in Oleander's heart.

She had been longing for Wanda Beaver so long that she had lost any other goals in her life. Even her elderly mother, out in the Vercingetorix Nursing Home, worried about her, when she remembered who she was.

"When are you going to forget this Beaver business?" old Mrs. Joy would say. "Look what Nikki's accomplished."

Nikki Joy, Oleander's travel agent sister, lived comfortably in a condominium in Indianapolis. She rarely visited old Mrs. Joy. "What would be the use?" she said to Oleander on the phone.

"You could call before you came to see if she was lucid," Oleander said.

"By the time I got there she'd forget me again," Nikki said. "It's pointless. Besides, she thinks I'm there, and that's just as good."

It was true that old Mrs. Joy believed that Nikki spent her afternoons sitting in the next bed, knitting. "Nikki and I watched 'Edge of Night' today," she'd say to Oleander. She turned to the next bed, which was often empty, and frowned. "Now where'd she go to? I suppose she went to the toilet. Oleander, you think you could sneak in some cigs?"

Oleander had a vision of the future for herself and Wanda Beaver. She and Wanda would get off the bus after a long day of detasseling and head home together to a big old house, not unlike the house old Mrs. Joy had grown up in in Tell City, which Oleander had loved to visit as a child. Oleander would open cans of smoked oysters, and she and Wanda Beaver would sit on the back steps eating oysters and drinking cherry Cokes as the fireflies came out and the trees vibrated with the droning of the cicadas and a hot blanket of night dropped over the town.

If it were up to Oleander, she would spend all year in the fields, tugging off corn tassels, as long as Wanda Beaver appeared to her now and then and said, "Nice rows, Oleander."

"Why, Wanda, thank you," Oleander would reply. "But you'll catch your death in that bikini. Here. Take my —" And she would quickly slip out of her own shirt, or sweatshirt, or down jacket, depending on the weather, and drape it over Wanda's goose-bumpled golden shoulders. The jacket would hang to her knees, loose and big as a tent.

"Why, Oleander," Wanda would say, looking at her as if for the first time. "You're absolutely right. I *was* cold." And she would continue on down the row, humming the tune Oleander had been humming when she arrived.

But detasseling was a purely seasonal job, lasting only a few weeks, and then Oleander went back to her full-time position at the Institute for the Study of American Sexual Appetite, where she worked in the Library of Desire. She was the Processing Clerk; every acquisition passed through her hands. She accessioned, stamped, measured, and recorded it all, and entered into the computer the descriptions that the cataloger scrawled on the accompanying forms.

The cataloger was a pale man named Will Middleton, who was an acknowledged expert on sexual models and paraphernalia, not only among the library staff but among the scientific staff of the Institute, and it was not unusual for visiting sexologists to be brought into the Cataloging Department to discuss the provenance or proper usage of newly identified sexual objects. Will Middleton had completed all the course work for a Ph.D. and even written a dissertation entitled "Nuances in the Recording of Sexual Idiosyncrasy: A Vision of Realia," but in the end he had been unable to face his orals board. He had never gotten his degree, but the administration had let him keep his job anyway.

During the seventies the Library had been a hotbed of activity, with new material in every conceivable medium flowing in at a steady pace. During the eighties, though, a precipitous drop in federal funding had coincided with decreasing academic interest in sexual activity, and every department had been forced to lay off not only support staff but professionals. Now, as the nineties slouched toward the millennium, Oleander Joy and Will Middleton were the only employees in Cataloging.

Will Middleton never talked about his life outside the Library, but he paid keen attention when Oleander came back after summer vacation and spoke of hers. He would take a bite of sandwich and then sit very still as Oleander described the busload of chattering teenaged girls, the raw-silk texture of a corn tassel, the weight of the midsummer sun on her shoulders, and the sun's slow slide over Wanda Beaver's long bikini-clad body. When Oleander blinked, and came out of her dream of

Wanda Beaver, she realized that Will Middleton had finished his entire sandwich without chewing.

"Oleander," he said now, "you're not getting any younger. What are you going to do about Wanda Beaver?"

A piece of Oleander's own sandwich stuck in her throat at his words, and she coughed for a while and had a long drink of water before she was able to speak. "Will," she said, "I'm not one to rush into things."

"It's all very well to laugh," he said, "but a lifetime of inaction is hardly worth the time, is it?"

"It's more like a lifetime of devotion, Will. Something quite different," Oleander said slowly.

Will leaned forward, shaking his head. "Are you going to hang there in suspended animation for the rest of your life?"

Oleander imagined herself dangling like an oversized piñata from the ceiling of the reference room, turning slowly in the infinitesimal breeze from the fans inside the computers, gazing helplessly down at the professors of sex who were tapping away at the keyboards of the online catalog. Probably no one would ever look up. She could bob gently above them forever.

She realized that Will was waiting for her answer, staring at her, his eyes huge and pale behind his plastic spectacles. "What?" she said.

Will sighed and sat back. "It's a good thing we're the best of friends, Oleander," he said. "Otherwise it would be very hard for me to work with you."

"I know," she said. "I would have trouble, too."

But she had been faking distraction: Will's words had

lodged in her brain. "Will," she said later that afternoon, "I think you are like the pot calling the kettle black."

Will Middleton looked up from the incunabulum he was examining. "Have you ever thought that perhaps the pot has a certain insight into the quality of blackness?"

"Are you saying," Oleander said, after pondering this for a moment, "that you live an empty life?"

Will gazed out the window behind her, where a ginkgo tree glowed in the afternoon sun. "Perhaps I'm saying," he said, so softly that Oleander had to lean toward him to catch the words, "that I have spent my life in a condition of unrequited longing."

"Why, Will," Oleander said. "I had no idea."

"Of course not," he said. "You're obsessed, and that's the nature of obsession. To be caught up so deeply that nothing but the object of the obsession exists for you. It's a disease."

"Love is not a disease," Oleander said.

"Love takes many forms," he said. "If it didn't, we'd be out of work."

They *were* the best of friends, but only within the walls of the Library of Desire. Oleander had never seen Will Middleton in the outside world; she had never imagined that there might be more to his story than met the eye. That afternoon as she unpacked boxes of books and plastic models and videotapes and magazines and piled them on the cart beside Will Middleton's desk, she watched him pick up each object, assign a classification number to it, and move on to the next one. He handled everything with the same detachment; nothing really caught his interest. He was so very pale, and his glasses were so thick!

Surely a person like Will Middleton could never experience the same sort of longing that Oleander felt for Wanda Beaver.

Old Mrs. Joy used to tell her daughters that time went faster as a woman aged. "It seems just yesterday," Mrs. Joy would say, "that the two of you were babies, in your little blond pigtails and little smocked dresses." Nikki and Oleander would roll their eyes at each other behind their mother's back, and sigh, and go on watching television, or eating, or doing each other's nails.

Over the years, though, the maternal mutterings had sunk in, and Oleander had fully expected time to begin to pass more swiftly, the world to spin more rapidly on its axis, and winters to pass in the blink of an eye. But what Mrs. Joy had not made clear was that only selected pieces of time rushed by. It was the summers in the corn that were gone before they had gotten well started; the rest of the year—the long autumnal dying, the colorless, lifeless winter, the spring that crawled out of the frozen earth at a snail's pace—went on and on and on as if time had been stretched beyond human imagination.

By early winter the ginkgo trees had lost their golden leaves and stood denuded outside the Library of Desire, glistening in the cold gray rain. This was the time of year when Oleander felt most hopeless. The next detasseling season was months ahead in an uncertain future, and the last was fast receding into the past. Now she had to go into the stacks and stand perfectly still, close her eyes, and hold her breath before she could summon up the beads of sweat on Wanda Beaver's forehead, the little prickles of dark stubble on her shaved thighs,

7

the gap where her prominent hips held her bikini bottom away from the tan skin of her stomach. Then, with the total Wanda Beaver spread-eagled against her eyelids, Oleander breathed deeply, and could almost feel the hard dry clods of earth underfoot and hear the sinister drone of flies from a nearby hog pen.

But she couldn't keep it up for long; a distant door would slam, or a student would wheel a truck of books into her aisle and start shoving them onto the shelves, or a sex researcher would sidle past, the soles of her boots making just enough noise that she jolted Oleander out of the past and drove Wanda Beaver farther into it. Then Oleander would sigh and clomp back down the corridor to her office, with such a dark cold hand of despair clutching at her heart that she was sure she would die before detasseling season rolled around again.

At such times Will Middleton would watch her closely as he pretended to analyze a newly acquired film on the VCR, and when she sat down at her desk and stared listlessly out the window, he would ask, with what might have been sympathy, "Thinking about the Beave again?"

Oleander sighed and nodded.

Will Middleton leaned back in his chair and crossed his arms. "How much do you know about this person, anyway?"

"I know enough," Oleander said.

"Is she married?" Will said. "Does she have children? What does she do in the winter?"

"These are superficial concerns," Oleander said.

Will Middleton leaned forward, his eyes large and wavery through his lenses. "Supposing," he said, "she were to fall in love?"

"With whom?" Oleander said.

"Anyone," he said. "Some man."

Oleander considered this. Wanda Beaver was so attractive, it *was* surprising that she hadn't ever married. Before Oleander's reluctant eyes there appeared the image of Wanda Beaver married to one of the detasseling foremen, or to someone who worked out at the steel recycling plant, someone with plenty of money and a hairy chest.

"Sure, baby, you can have anything your skinny little heart desires," the unknown man drooled over Wanda Beaver's bare shoulders. "Sure, you can have that run-down ol' place in Tell City. We'll fix it up real nice."

And there they were, the hairy man and Wanda Beaver, packed like Okies into the man's old Chevrolet, driving out of town on Route 142, looking straight ahead down the road toward Tell City. When they got there they got out of the car and walked right up the steps of old Mrs. Joy's house, with old Mrs. Joy as a little girl still sitting there in a pinafore. Hairy walked right into the house and began to live there with Wanda Beaver, when it was Oleander who should have been doing it instead.

She felt as if she had stepped into another dimension, where she could see things from an entirely different angle than she ever had before. Wanda Beaver could marry a hairy man at any time.

"Will," she said, "what should I do?"

He reached over and tapped the INTERRUPT button, leaving the video to flicker impotently on the screen. "Oleander," he said, "what is it you want?"

Oleander stared helplessly at him, trying to think of a way to phrase it. It had to do with the nature of desire itself, and the condition of completion. When she saw Wanda in the corn, her protuberant teeth gleaming in the sun, it was as if Oleander's skin went suddenly empty, the way a papier-mâché sculpture is suddenly empty when the balloon inside it is pricked by a pin. Just as a sculpture hardens into the shape of the balloon, her skin had taken on the shape of her desire; and the knowledge that there was no way of fulfilling her desire filled her with both ecstasy and despair.

But Will's words had made her realize that she was in danger of losing everything. So long as her imagination had lived within definite boundaries, she had been full of a certain kind of hope, an elation at the limitlessness of possibility. Now the suggestion of an alternate reality had torn a jagged, dangerous hole in the thin membrane around her life. Her condition had changed. She could hope, but she could not pretend.

"I just want to be happy," she said.

Will Middleton stood up and began to pace back and forth across the office. "Happiness is a byproduct," he said. "An accident. A result." He looked sideways at her. "You don't want happiness, you want Wanda Beaver."

"It's the same thing," Oleander said.

"Oh, Oleander," he said, "after all these years here, haven't you figured it out? The difference between passion and happiness, desire and fulfillment, the object and the pursuit?"

She put her hands over her ears. "I don't know what you're talking about," she said. "I'm not an intellectual." And she closed her eyes and sat hunched over as his voice droned on.

What did he know about love? All he loved was his cataloging work; he was as far removed from reality as it was possible to be. He spent his days categorizing love into erotica, or sexuality, or lust, describing it in rigidly defined terms, and popping it into a computer database. Why, Will Middleton spent his time trying to objectify love and make it mean the same thing to everyone, which led to its meaning nothing to anyone.

I'm not the one living in a dreamworld, Oleander thought, and she smiled as she imagined herself floating high over a cornfield in late July, gazing down at herself among the teenaged girls working the rows, their smooth-muscled arms reaching overhead to pluck the tassel from each stalk. There was nothing more real than the weight of the Midwestern sun on your back in late July, or even the helpless, defeated feeling that filled you as you inched your way through rows of wet corn after a week of thunderstorms, the mud sucking hungrily at your sneakers, drops of cold water and small sticky specks of corn germ shaking off and sticking to your skin and your glasses when you reached up for a tassel. Nothing more real than, in the middle of such a dismal day, the sudden stab of pleasure in your heart at the sight of a dripping Wanda Beaver at the end of the row.

"I won't last forever," old Mrs. Joy had often said, and as winter turned the corner toward spring, it became all too clear that her words had been prophetic. She became vaguer and vaguer, until at last it was evident that she would never again remember who Oleander was.

"It's as if she's already gone," Oleander said to Nikki on the telephone.

"She's been gone for years," Nikki said.

"But she's always *been* there," Oleander said. "Sundays and Wednesdays, she was always waiting for me."

Nikki snorted. "She didn't care if you were there or not."

"How do you know?" Oleander said. "You never bothered to visit her."

"If she's happy in a dreamworld, leave her there. I've got better things to do than force people to face reality."

"That's not the point," Oleander said.

Nikki sighed. "You're just like her."

"I am?" Oleander said.

"Take this Wanda Beaver," Nikki said. "She's a figment of your imagination. You've never even spoken to her."

"Of course I have." Oleander glared at the telephone. "When we're out in the fields we talk all the time."

"Okay, okay," Nikki said. "Just remember, you're not a spring chicken. And that library's a dead end, too."

"It's an important research institution," Oleander said.

"Sure," Nikki said. "Those who can't do, teach; and those who can't teach, do research."

"You don't know what you're talking about," Oleander said. "They're world-renowned experts."

"Expert shmexpert," Nikki said. "Take my advice. Get out into the real world before it's too late." Oleander heard her puffing on her cigarette and could almost smell the smoke drifting through the receiver. "Let's just hope she doesn't use up our inheritance in hospital bills. I'd like to get to Paris once in my life."

As her mother faded, Oleander at times felt strangely lighthearted, as if the string that had tethered her to earth all her life was fraying, and once it snapped nothing would remain to keep her from soaring away. But at other times the threat of freedom hung heavy on her heart. Day after day she plodded along the streets through the melting snow and down the steps of the Library of Desire, and she felt that no one in the world would notice or care if she went in the door and never came out again.

Walking along, she thought deeply about what Nikki had said. Maybe Will Middleton was a cataloger in the Library of Desire because he couldn't function in the real world. If those who couldn't do research did cataloging, what did that say about those who just processed item after item, connecting to nothing at all?

For so long she had thought that she was working in the Library of Desire just so she could afford to spend her summer vacation in her real life, in the cornfields with Wanda Beaver. Was she fooling herself? Could it be that the truth was something else—that she stayed in the Library because she was afraid to plunge into the fields of life wholeheartedly?

What could she do? If she approached Wanda Beaver—if she *spoke* to her—she risked losing not just her detasseling job, but the life she had built around it. If only there was something that would give her the answer, tell her what to do. Nothing or something? That's what it boiled down to. Either way the risk was the same.

She was so deep in thought that she walked right into Ruthie Cline. The impact knocked her to the ground.

"Are you all *right*?" Ruthie shrieked. "Have you broken a *hip*?"

"Ruthie, I just turned forty, for God's sake," Oleander said, letting Ruthie help her up.

"I'm not concerned with your age," Ruthie said. "Oh my God, is that you, Oleander?"

"Who did you think it was, Noam Chomsky?" Oleander said crossly. She shook off Ruthie's clutching hand.

"I thought it was some poor old soul who couldn't get up," Ruthie said. "If you didn't want any help, you should have stood up."

"Thank you, Ruthie," Oleander said. "What are you up to these days, anyway?"

"About five five," Ruthie said. "Ha ha. Remember, I was such a jokester in school? I still am, Oleander. I don't think people really change much, do you?"

Oleander shrugged. "You didn't recognize *me*."

"Well, you weren't always lying on the sidewalk," Ruthie said. "And Oleander, pardon me for saying this, but you have put on a little weight, haven't you?"

"I really don't know," Oleander said. "It's not something I pay much attention to."

"Same old Oleander," Ruthie said. "Lost in a daydream. Still detasseling with Wanda Beaver? Ha ha."

Oleander frowned. "As a matter of fact, I am."

Ruthie shook her head. "Oleander," she said, "what would you do with Wanda Beaver if you had her?"

And Oleander began to tell Ruthie Cline about the house in Tell City where her mother, old Mrs. Joy, had grown up, and where Oleander and her sister, Nikki, had spent so many summer vacations before their grandparents died and the house was sold. She told her about the wide front porch with the lattice where brilliant red roses had climbed; about the peeling white paint; about the dim hallway that smelled of dust and cats and lilacs as you stood just inside the door waiting for your eyes to adjust to the dark; about the huge, sparsely furnished rooms with no reading lamps where she and Nikki wandered while their mother sat on the porch drinking gin and lemonade with *her* mother.

And she told her of her dream: that she would take Wanda Beaver to live in the old house, and they would lie out in the yard on summer afternoons letting their skin darken and burn, and as the sun finally began to drop behind the snowball bushes and shadows slowly crept toward them across the lawn, they would go inside and take ice-cold bottles of beer from the refrigerator and stand together in the dim kitchen chugging the beer, which would trickle over Wanda Beaver's upturned chin and down her neck, mingling with the sweat that stood in the little hollow between her clavicles, and drip down her chest into the dark space in the center of her bikini top and out again on the other side.

Ruthie closed her mouth. "That's all?"

Oleander opened her eyes. "Isn't that enough?"

"It seems quite innocent," Ruthie said.

Oleander sighed. "Maybe it wouldn't be enough for her."

"If it's enough for you," Ruthie said, "it might very well be enough for her."

In later years Oleander could not pinpoint the exact moment when she decided to act, or exactly what pushed her over the edge toward action. It might have been Will Middleton's prodding; it might have been her mother's gradual slide toward death; it might have been Nikki Joy's harsh remarks about the lack of substance in Oleander's life.

Or it might have been the miraculous encounter with Ruthie Cline. For as Oleander stood there staring at her, Ruthie fished a business card out of her pocketbook. "I'm in real estate now, Oleander. Tell City's out of my territory, but there are some real nice manufactured homes out in South Towne Village."

Oleander stared at the card Ruthie had thrust at her.

"Interest rates are terrific these days," Ruthie said, shrewdly watching Oleander's face. "But they could go up any day."

Oleander looked from the card to Ruthie's face. "I don't have a down payment right now," she said, "but I might have at any time."

Ruthie nodded. "It's the American dream," she said. "It's what everyone wants in her heart of hearts."

And as if there were miracles, it was spring. The pale days stretched out longer and longer, flocks of migrating songbirds stopped to rest in the flowering ginkgo trees, and business picked up in the Library of Desire as researchers ventured out of their offices, excited once again at the concept of love.

All winter the image of Wanda Beaver had shrunk and grown fainter, and Oleander had squinted and concentrated hard just to picture her smile, but now, in spring, she had only to blink and Wanda Beaver grinned at her. She smelled her suntan lotion in the shower, she heard her voice as she walked to work, and all day she caught glimpses of Wanda Beaver in the Library of Desire, leaning over the reference copy of the *Kama Sutra*, disappearing into the locked stacks of Early American Erotica, flickering across a TV screen in the wet carrel where a social work student was watching a clinical video.

As spring turned to summer and the corn in the fields outside of town shot skyward, Oleander's heart rose to a spot high in her chest, just below her neck, where it lay swollen, pounding irregularly, cutting off the air to her lungs. She had trouble concentrating on her work; several times Will Middleton had to ask her to re-enter data she had mistyped, or relabel the rubber Victorian appliances a wealthy benefactress had left to the Library.

"I just hope I'm doing the right thing," Oleander said as she cleaned off her desk the day before her vacation started.

"It's better to have loved and lost than never to have loved at all," Will said.

"Oh, for heaven's sake," she said, "I *do* love. I don't need to lose."

"You love," he said softly, "but until you *are* loved in return, you have no idea what love can be."

She looked over at him and saw that he had taken off his glasses, and that the thick lashes surrounding his violet eyes were the color of ripening peaches. She felt a rush of affection for him; poor Will Middleton, her good friend, who had patiently listened to her and advised her for so many years. A man with nothing and no one, who had not exactly *failed* in life, but had sort of given up, and settled into a safe little slot, and spent his days classifying the experiences of the world around him, never daring to have any of his own.

"Will," she said, "you once said that you were full of unrequited longing. What for?"

It might have been the moment Will Middleton had been waiting for. At her words a light might have gone on in his pale eyes, and his breath begun to come a little faster in his thin and hairless chest, as his own unspoken hopes and deeply concealed desires began to edge toward the light of day.

But as he looked at Oleander, he saw that her thoughts had already skipped beyond him, beyond the walls of the Library of Desire, and out to the cornfield where Wanda Beaver waited. "A Ph.D.," he said, and he was not surprised when she didn't even hear him.

At five-thirty in the morning Oleander climbed onto the bus with the other detasselers. She listened idly to the giggling teenagers and gazed out the window as the bus passed the familiar schools and houses, the Institute where Will Middleton would soon be hard at work, the Vercingetorix Nursing Home where her mother lay unaware of what would happen to her daughter today. The sun was behind the trees and its light was still kind, its heat tender, and a sweet haze lay on the fields of tall lush corn. She wished that the ride would never end. She wished the bus would eternally travel through the morning light along a two-lane road, between endless fields of corn, and that starlings would soar in great unmolested swarms over the fields forever.

But the bus rolled into someone's barnyard and stopped in front of a gleaming steel barn. Oleander moved with the teenagers down the steps and saw Wanda Beaver, in shorts and a T-shirt, standing with the other crew bosses, talking to the farmer. Wanda was nodding, her hands on her hips, her eyes now and then drifting away from the faces of the people she stood with and out over the field into which the detasselers would soon plunge.

Oleander started toward her, but she thought better of it and made her way to the far side of the group of teenagers. Wanda sent the girls into the field, one per row, until Oleander was the only one left.

"Okay, Oleander," Wanda Beaver said. "Go for it."

Now or never, Oleander thought, and with a pounding heart she took her life in her hands and bravely said, "Wanda?"

"Yo," Wanda Beaver said, looking at her as if she had never really noticed her before.

Oleander knew that this was the moment she had been moving inevitably toward for forty years. Everything she knew of love was gathered there at the edge of the cornfield. All that she had learned, everything she had experienced had prepared her for this moment, and yet she felt so unprepared. She wasn't ready. How to begin? I love you? Howsabout shacking up? You are the most miraculous thing in my life, and I want to live with you?

"Do you own your home?" Oleander said.

Wanda Beaver snickered. "You think I'm made of money or what?"

"It's the American dream," Oleander said, "and my dream, too."

Wanda Beaver looked at her watch. "My cousin's in real estate," she said. "I'll tell her to give you a call."

"Oh," Oleander said, a little disconcerted. "But not just that." She took a deep breath and stepped forward. "I have something to tell you."

Wanda Beaver felt an entirely new sensation in her solar plexus as Oleander came toward her. "Jiminy," she said.

Afterwards, it was this moment that Oleander would put on personal reserve in the Library of Desire, to be checked out, carried off into the dark stacks on the third floor, and perused again and again: the oil glistening on Wanda Beaver's body, its sweet coconut fragrance rising like steam from her thighs; the morning sunlight, thick with promised heat, that coated the heavy green leaves of corn; the weightless little white clouds skipping across the sky, the black shape of a hawk circling slowly beneath them; the thin bright light of understanding that had begun to dawn in Wanda Beaver's eyes; and the fragile, frightening possibility that the next soft brown tassel that Oleander touched would hold the love she had been seeking for so long.

Ooh, Baby, Baby

"I don't know that I can do this for an entire week," RayBob said, staring at the long leather gloves JoAnne had left on the kitchen counter. Nearby were a syringe, a large brown bottle of medicine, and a pile of catfood cans.

Beside him Carl the Human Dog grinned, stringy saliva rolling from the corner of his mouth. "I'll deal with him," Carl said in his stupid human voice.

"Don't tempt me," RayBob said. He frowned at the two coffee cups in the sink. "How sweet," he said. "How fucking domestic." He turned and stomped back out through the living room and down the hall. He had planned to stay out of the bedroom, but he might as well get it over with. He flung open the door.

She'd bought a new bedspread, but it was the same bed. *His* bed. He himself had rigged the bathroom faucet so they could run a hose out of the bathtub to fill it. It was probably still the same water. Guido was sleeping on RayBob's original water.

RayBob laughed mirthlessly and stalked over to the bureau. There was a picture of him, the one where he looked a little like

Carl Sagan, his hair falling across his forehead from way back on his head. He moved the photo to the edge of the bureau so that it stared at the bed.

"So," he said, picking up another one, "you must be Guido." A swarthy man smiled at him with more teeth than any one person could ever use. He had deep-set dark eyes, and his abundant hair was brushed straight back from his face to reveal a striking widow's peak. In one ear he wore a tiny gold ring. RayBob stuck him behind a jewelry box.

He flopped down on the bed and lay staring at himself in the mirror overhead, jerking his hips now and then to keep the wave motion going. It made him feel funny to know that JoAnne kept a picture of him in her bedroom and that Guido apparently didn't mind. *That* was a self-confident man.

Back in the kitchen Chill the Cat crouched on top of the leather gloves, pretending his eyes were closed. "Okay, catface, let's get this show on the road," RayBob said, pushing him off the gloves.

Chill shrieked and slashed at him with fully extended claws.

"Chill *loves* you," JoAnne had said on the phone. "I trust you."

"Used to be the other way round," RayBob said.

"Oh, Rayby, please," she'd said.

"Rayby?" someone in the background said. "What is he, some kind of disease?"

"Is that Guido?" RayBob said. "Look, JoAnne, nip this in the bud. A Guido from New Jersey is bad news."

"We said we'd stay friends, remember?" she said. "You *are* Chill's original father."

"Not the original original," he said.

"Guido's giving a paper," JoAnne said. "We're making it a vacation."

"Why are you telling me this?" RayBob said.

"Chill," she said.

For years she had insisted that Chill the Cat's ulcer was caused by stress, and that if RayBob would just get rid of the Human Dog, Chill would be able to relax and digest his meals properly. But Carl had moved out when RayBob did, and Chill still required daily doses of Tagamet to keep his food traveling in one direction through his digestive system.

RayBob opened the bottle and filled the syringe with the colorless liquid. Then he yanked the gloves out from under Chill, who sprang from the counter and disappeared under the stove. RayBob shook his head in disgust and stomped back into the living room.

"He should be put to sleep," he said. He sat down on the sofa and put his feet up on the coffee table and started rolling a joint.

Carl's breathing intensified briefly, but his eyes remained closed.

"She loves him, though," RayBob said. He knew he was a pushover. He saw himself as a large, man-shaped marshmallow, dented all over where women had poked at him to make him do things. The thought made him hungry.

In the refrigerator was one of those little logs of herbed goat cheese. "Chèvre," she used to whisper to him in the dark. It drove him crazy. He found some bread and a bottle of red wine and went back into the living room. Carl, not bothering to lift his head from the floor, watched with one eye as RayBob finished the wine. They could hear Chill scraping away at the cat box in the guest bathroom.

The next morning the odor of Chill's deposit lingered, so RayBob took his shampoo and walked naked down the hall to use JoAnne's shower. The sight of Guido's toothbrush in the slot where his had once hung made him feel even worse than the coffee cups had. As he took a long shower he noticed a thin line of dark matter on the grout between some tiles, so he scrubbed at it with Guido's toothbrush. It made him feel a little better.

JoAnne called before he left for work. "Is everything okay? It isn't too hard for you, is it?"

"What are you talking about?" RayBob said. "Chill loves me."

"*That* I know," she said. "I meant emotionally."

"Carl crapped at that same bus stop. It was like old times."

"He was such a sweet puppy," JoAnne said. "We had some good times, didn't we?"

"Speaking of good times, where'd Guido get all those shirts, Smith and Hawken?" RayBob said.

"Snooping won't hurt anyone but you, RayBob," JoAnne said. "Did Chill take his medicine?"

"And proved its efficacy," RayBob said.

When he left Chill was curled in his old leather chair. Carl lay on his back under the air conditioner, exposing his genitals to the cold air. His eyelids hung open on his upside-down head, revealing a crazy slice of white in each eye, and his black lips hung away from his teeth. RayBob smacked him lightly on the bare skin of his stomach. "Have a terrific day, guys," he said.

It was not unusual for people to recognize RayBob when he went out on a call. More than once he'd been strapping someone onto a gurney, or wrapping the cuff around an upper arm, when the person in crisis opened her eyes and saw RayBob's face hovering above her own. The eyes would slowly focus, and a light would come into them. "Rock 'n' roll heaven," more than one patient had whispered.

RayBob loved to see the light in the eyes—it was the best part of his job—but he hated it when people thought he was dead. He would shake his head. "You're still on Planet Earth," he'd say, watching the seconds blink by on his watch as he held the patient's wrist. "You and me both."

It was amazing how sick some people could be and still ask for his autograph. He had signed not only casts and bandages but a sneaker that was removed from a nearly severed foot and several pieces of underwear. "Here," a tearful wife, or girlfriend, or even mother would finally say, after a man on the verge of death had begged for RayBob's autograph and RayBob had searched futilely through his pockets for a piece of paper. The woman would turn away, and when she turned back she'd be holding out her slip, or her bra. What did a patient think when he woke up, RayBob wondered, and there in the little nightstand beside his hospital bed was his wife's bra, one cup inscribed with the signature of a rock star he'd thought was dead? Or when a patient died, and his mother finally, months later, was able to look at the effects she'd carried home from the hospital in a plastic bag, and there with his glasses and a pack of Camels and the unopened condom from his wallet was the bloodstained sole of an Etonics Trainer, with *RayBob Van Gelder* scrawled across it?

"I'd rather wake up to see Paul McCartney leaning over me," Melanie said. "Unzipping my zippers, putting his hand on parts of my body where the blood rushes close to the surface."

"You make him sound like a pervert," RayBob said. "P. McCartney, Ghoul."

They were sitting in the hospital cafeteria having a cup of coffee. RayBob liked hospitals. He knew that mistakes were made, and doctors were only human, but at least if an accident occurred in a hospital, there would be plenty of people around who would *take charge*.

Melanie sighed. "I should have gone to medical school," she said. "I'd be doing less of the same thing for more money."

"Your net would be less, though," RayBob said. "Thousands for malpractice insurance."

"Ah, but I'd have prestige," she said.

"Honey, you got prestige when you're riding in that buggy with me," RayBob said, leaning across the table and seizing her hand.

"Cool it, Elvis," Melanie said. She shook his hand off. "How's the baby-sitting going?"

"I don't know why I ever agreed to it," he said, shaking his head. "What possessed me?"

"You are still hung up on that woman," Melanie said.

"You're hoping she'll remember what a wonderful father you were to her cat and dump the professor."

"I don't think she will," RayBob said sadly. "I think she thinks of me as a brother now."

"Let it be a lesson to you," Melanie said. "How many people do you know who are really friends with their exes?"

"I can't even begin to count them," RayBob said.

"That's because you flunked negative numbers," she said, standing up and reaching for her jacket. "I haven't seen Tiffany's alleged father in three years, and I am a happy woman. Come on, let's go save another life."

RayBob came home tired. He took the Human Dog for his walk and then flung himself down in a chair with a beer. "Chill," he called, "do your own medicine, okay?"

Chill, who was in the kitchen sitting on the leather gloves, did not respond.

RayBob felt the tension of his workday slide away as he drank, and when he emptied the bottle he leaned back and closed his eyes. The truth was, he was disappointed. He had hoped that by staying in JoAnne's house, taking care of their old cat, watching TV with Carl where they'd watched TV so many cozy evenings in the past, he'd feel close to JoAnne again. It wasn't quite what Melanie thought—he didn't necessarily want JoAnne to dump Guido—but he wanted to know that they were still connected in some way; that the little family they'd been— RayBob, JoAnne, Chill the Cat, and Carl the Human Dog—was still a family.

The phone rang. He picked up the receiver and said, "You know, you don't have to call every night. Chill doesn't expect it."

"It's for my own peace of mind," JoAnne said. "How's my baby?"

"He doesn't love me anymore," RayBob said. "What'd you do today?"

"He shows his affection in strange ways," JoAnne said. "I shopped all morning and lay out by the pool all afternoon. Do you know how much easier it is to spend money when you're not on your own territory?"

"Do you know how prevalent skin cancer is?" RayBob said. "Did Guido give his oral report?"

"Yes," she said. "Now he can relax." She held her hand over the receiver and then said, "He says you can borrow any of his shirts you want to."

"What a guy," RayBob said. "Tell him they're b-b-b-beautiful."

The next morning when RayBob reached for the gloves, Chill drove one of his claws faster than lightning through the skin of RayBob's wrist and ripped it open down to the elbow, and as RayBob hopped around the kitchen clutching his arm, his mouth stretched wide in a silent scream, Chill sat up on his haunches with both front paws poised for action if RayBob even dreamed of trying again.

"Shit!" RayBob finally hissed, and he held his arm away from his chest to look at the damage. Blood oozed from a thin line down his arm and dripped onto the floor. His uniform shirt was smeared with his own blood.

Carl the Human Dog wandered into the kitchen looking hopeful. "Jesus Christ, Carl, there's nothing here for you," RayBob yelled, and Carl put his ears down and turned away, trying to tuck his little stub between his legs.

Chill settled down onto all four limbs again and folded his front paws under his chest. He closed his eyes.

RayBob took off his clothes again and stepped into JoAnne's shower, and let the hot water wash the blood away until finally it stopped oozing. When he was drying himself off with what he hoped was Guido's towel, he noticed that the water was sitting in the shower stall, hardly going down the drain at all. Still naked, he got the plumber's helper from behind the toilet— he'd put it there himself—and plunged away, until with a sad sucking noise the water began to disappear. For good measure he poured a capful of lye down after it.

Then he bandaged his arm, put on some clothes, and marched out to the kitchen to confront Chill. Chill did not put up much of a fight. RayBob thought he sensed the fury in his former dad. He knew when to leave well enough alone.

"I know that kind of wound," Melanie said when she saw the long stripe of gauze on RayBob's arm. "Either you tried to commit suicide or Chill let you know who was boss."

"Same thing," RayBob said. "Go near that cat, you take your life in your hands."

"Next time, board him," she said. "JoAnne would never know."

"Hell," RayBob said. "I'll just fake giving him the medicine. She'll never know that either."

"You're too conscientious for that," Melanie said, shaking her head.

The whole day was depressing. They had three contract runs, all of them transporting ancient people from longtime homes to their final berths in extended-care facilities.

"I'll tell you one more time," Melanie said as they pulled out of the parking lot at Oak Lane Manor. "If Tiffany tries to stick me in a home, just lose me on the way."

"You think that's what Mr. Santos wanted?" RayBob said. "To be dumped somewhere along the beltway?"

"Mr. Santos didn't want anything except a one-way ticket on the eternity express. So the baby-sitting's almost done?"

"One more night," RayBob said. "Then it's good-bye, Chill."

"Well, for your sake, I hope it's good-bye, JoAnne. That woman has taken advantage of you since day one."

RayBob sighed. "We had some good times, though. We were happy for a while."

"Then just leave it there," Melanie said. "Remember the good times and light out for some new territory."

RayBob closed his eyes and tried to imagine himself lighting out. Instead he saw Mr. Santos, who opened his eyes, lifted his head and shoulders from the hospital bed, and looked around. Then he reached out from under the sheet and unstrapped himself, and sitting up he swung his skinny little legs over the side. His legs were like coat hangers that had been straightened out and were rippled where once they'd swept straight and shining from one tense curve to the next. But they held Mr. Santos upright when he stood, and when he'd clutched the sheet up around his chest, they carried him in a quick scurry out of his new room at Oak Lane Manor, down the green hall, and through the wide glass doors into the street. The last RayBob saw of him, old Mr. Santos was running down Wilmington Boulevard, blinking in the sunlight and now and then giving a little leap into the air as he went.

"We'll be rolling in around noon," JoAnne said. "You don't really have to stay tonight."

"I've gotta clean up," RayBob said. "Throw out the roaches and redeem the returnables. Besides, I'm already in my jammies."

"Well, I hope you've got the curtains closed," she said. "RayBob, I really do appreciate your taking care of Chill this way."

"Anything for you, JoAnne," RayBob said mellifluously.

"I know you think you're kidding," she said, "but I also know you really mean that."

"Right," he said. "I don't think Chill wants me back, though. He's locked himself in the bathroom."

"Isn't he something," JoAnne said. "Are you going to still be there tomorrow? I just want to know."

"I'd like to get a gander at Guido," RayBob said. "Hey, good line. Get a gander at Guido," he sang, "and give a goose to JoAnne."

"When are you going to grow up," JoAnne said, but he thought she was laughing. "Yes or no?"

"You can't answer 'when' with a yes or a no," RayBob said, but when he started to sing it, she hung up.

In the morning he stripped the sheets off the sofa bed and

dumped them in the washing machine, and then went into JoAnne's bathroom for Guido's towels. Chill was crouched in the shower, staring intently down the drain.

"No more torture from me," RayBob said. "You're JoAnne's baby now."

Chill made a small sound but otherwise paid no attention. RayBob pulled the towels off the racks, and then he reached into the shower to retrieve the blue washcloth. He looked down past Chill's head into the drain and saw a hand.

He gasped, and Chill started and stared up at him as the gasp echoed around inside the shower. RayBob backed away and sat down on the toilet, holding the towels up in front of him, and took a couple of deep breaths. His heart felt small and square, as if the shock had compressed it into a little black box. He stood up and tiptoed over to look again.

A tiny pink hand was palm up against the grate covering the drain, as if it were trying to push it off. RayBob leaned closer and peered at it; the fingers were short and stubby, and he could almost see minute whorls. Suddenly Chill yowled. RayBob jumped a foot.

He went out and stood in the living room for a moment, staring out the window. He was used to emergencies; why had his mind gone completely blank? He was ashamed. He reached for the phone. "Melanie," he said into the receiver in a startlingly high voice, "do you think you could come over here?"

"Over where?" she said.

"JoAnne's house," he said. "The thing is, there's something in the shower."

"Dudududu," she sang in a Twilight Zone voice. "Norman Bates."

"Melanie, listen." RayBob noticed that his hand was shaking, and he clutched the receiver tighter. "It's a baby."

She was silent for a minute. "There's a baby in the shower," she said.

"It's in the *drain*," he whispered. "It's coming up through the drain."

"You having a flashback, RayBob?"

"Would you just come over?" The shaking seemed to have gotten into his voice. "I don't quite know what to do."

"Hello, Carl," Melanie said when RayBob opened the front door. She leaned over and scratched the itchy spot beside Carl's left ear. She stood up and looked at RayBob. "You are as pale as the proverbial."

"I feel like a fool," RayBob said.

"I am reserving judgment," she said, and she followed him down the hall and into the bedroom.

Chill sat on the pile of towels that RayBob had dropped on the floor. "Chill's been in there all week," RayBob said. "I didn't think anything of it. Carl, sit." He waited till Carl had sat and then he opened the bathroom door. They crept in.

"This is ridiculous," Melanie said, and she stepped in front of him and looked into the shower. She knelt down on hands and knees and leaned over. "Well," she said, "it ain't no Barbie doll."

RayBob sat down on the toilet. "I shouldn't have bothered you," he said. "It just weirded me out."

Melanie sat back on her knees and looked at him. "RayBob," she said, "it would be a surprise to anyone. Babies don't too often come up in the shower." She leaned toward it again, frowning. "Looks like about a fifteen-week fetus. Same development in the fingers. Somebody must have lost it and flushed it."

RayBob felt a little weak around the lips. "I guess we should get it out."

Melanie put her hand on his knee. "Why don't you let me do this?"

"I'm not *that* sensitive," he said in surprise. "It was just a shock for a moment."

"I don't mean that," she said. "It might be too personal, is all."

He stared at her. "Personal?"

"RayBob, you are still hooked on that woman."

RayBob, who had half risen from the toilet seat, dropped back down. "JoAnne?" he said, the last syllable escaping from his throat and squeaking up past his ears.

"Where do you think this baby came from?"

He hadn't thought about it. "You think she put a fetus down the shower?"

Melanie rolled her eyes. "Think," she said. "She probably flushed it, and then somehow it got into the wrong pipe. All the rain we been having."

"I don't think plumbing works that way," RayBob said. "Anyway, she'd never do something like that."

"See what I mean? Too close to home." She reached for the

sink and pulled herself up. "A desperate woman will do things you never dreamed of."

"Why would she be desperate? She's forty-five years old."

"Enough reason right there," Melanie said.

RayBob frowned. "Maybe we should wait. She'll be here by noon."

Melanie looked down at the hand in the drain and then at him. "You're the star of this show," she said. "You call the shots."

RayBob imagined himself waiting just inside the door as JoAnne walked in. "We found it," he hissed as he glided toward her with glowing, accusatory eyes. "The baby in your shower." He could see the look of horror on her face, and just as he reached out to touch her, she threw back her head and let out a blood-curdling scream.

"It might be easier on her if she didn't have to see it in there," he said.

"Easier on *her*," Melanie muttered. "I dare say it would."

RayBob found the toolbox under the kitchen sink, just where he'd left it. "I don't think those tools have been touched since I left," he said as he carried the screwdriver into the bedroom. "Guido probably wouldn't know a screwdriver if it stood up and bit him."

"English professors don't have to, RayBob." Melanie lay spread-eagled on the waterbed, staring up at herself in the mirror. She took off her glasses and squinted. "I would have to wear my glasses in bed if I wanted to see what was going on here."

"Melanie," RayBob said. "Can we please get this over with?" He went into the bathroom and knelt down in the shower.

The hand seemed to move slightly as he looked at it, as if the body attached to it was breathing in a deep sleep. He could almost hear a faint snoring, the kind of snoring babies do when they've got little colds, or when their heads are turned sideways enough to slightly close off their airways. Snoring down there in the cool damp drainpipe, tucked in under the stainless steel grate.

Melanie came into the room behind him.

"I put lye down there," RayBob whispered.

She put her hand on his shoulder and squeezed. "It's all right, RayBob. It never was alive."

He tried to clear his throat without making any noise and looked around at her. She held a large black garbage bag. "You're not going to put it in that?"

She looked at him blankly. "We don't exactly need a receiving blanket."

He shook his head. "You really have a way with words, Melanie."

"RayBob," she said, squatting down beside him, "at that stage of development, it's not much different from an appendix."

"I know it," he said. "It's just that little hand."

She nodded.

He struggled with the screwdriver for fifteen minutes before the screws finally gave way and reluctantly began to turn. Melanie's breathing became louder as she knelt beside him clutching the garbage bag. As he drew the last screw out of its bed, she let out her breath in a long low sigh.

RayBob lifted the grate away from the drain and the hand drifted up in slow motion from the dark pipe. "Oh, God," he said.

"Here," Melanie whispered, and she thrust at him the leather gloves he used for handling Chill.

RayBob pulled them on, thinking that never, in all the things he'd ever done, had his hands shaken so much. He was getting old. "Here goes," he said. He slid his right hand down into the pipe and took the fragile little arm between his thumb and forefinger. Barely able to feel it through the leather, he pulled as gently as he could. To his great relief the arm did not come off; instead the whole body behind it moved, and as he pulled, it slid easily up the strange cold canal into the light of day. Melanie shifted beside him, and he realized that he, too, was backing away, trying to keep it at arm's length. As he eased it out, he turned his hand to catch the whole thing in his cupped palm.

"Oh, my," Melanie said faintly.

Dark hair was plastered in wet globs all over its body. Its little eyes were closed tight, and its mouth was squeezed in a thin lipless line, giving it a grim, clenched-jaw look. The legs hung limply as RayBob lifted it.

"It's a possum," Melanie said. "A baby possum."

RayBob's squeezed-up heart suddenly expanded in a great flow of blood, and he let out a loud gush of breath. He laid the possum down on top of the garbage bag.

Melanie leaned heavily on his shoulder and pushed herself up. "I'm getting us a beer."

RayBob pulled off the gloves and crawled out of the bathroom on his hands and knees. He did not know if he would ever stand upright again. As he crept into the bedroom, Chill sprang toward the bathroom with gleaming eyes, but RayBob summoned enough energy to yank the door closed before Chill could reach it.

Carl danced around moofing delightedly as RayBob crawled across the room, and when RayBob climbed onto the bed, he threw himself down on his back on the floor and wriggled around, moaning in pleasure.

RayBob stared up at his reflection. He felt the way he had years ago when he'd had the mumps and lay in bed watching feverish visions of himself grow smaller and smaller at the end of a tunnel, and then with no warning zoom back up the tunnel larger than life. He looked at his face and could see nothing familiar about it; he was no one he'd ever known.

Melanie dropped down beside him, splashing them both with flying beerdrops, and they watched themselves bob and shake as the waterbed slowly calmed.

RayBob closed his eyes. "I'm such a fool."

"For thinking it was JoAnne's baby?"

He opened his eyes and stared at himself overhead. "For thinking it was mine."

"Yours?"

He shrugged. "We got together a couple of times after I moved out. It could have been."

"Jesus, RayBob," Melanie said. She lifted her head to take a drink and then lay back and crossed her arms over her chest. She stared at him in the mirror. "You ever want kids?"

"I don't know," he said. "Sure. We tried for a while. No dice."

"How about before JoAnne? You leave a string of little bastards behind you when your band went on tours?"

"Not that I ever heard," he said. "Anyway, I never had what you might call groupies. I wasn't exactly Mick Jagger."

"What a world," she said. "Tiffany ever tries anything like this, I'll kill her."

"Like what? Lying fully clothed on a waterbed?"

"You know what I'm talking about."

"Flushing possums?"

"When I think about it," she said, and she snickered.

"My son, the possum," RayBob said, and he started to laugh.

They lay shaking with laughter, churning the waterbed into convulsions, and whenever they managed to open their eyes and look up, they saw each other writhing and jiggling helplessly, which sent them off again. They laughed so hard and so long that RayBob didn't hear Carl barking in the living room, and didn't hear the front door open, and didn't hear any footsteps until he saw JoAnne standing beside the bed.

He held out his arms and cried, "The mother of my possum!"

Melanie shrieked and covered her face with her hands, pouring what was left of her beer into her hair.

JoAnne turned and headed toward the bathroom, but as her hand touched the doorknob, RayBob and Melanie both cried out, "No!"

"Don't go in there!" RayBob said, sitting up.

She turned and looked at them. "Why not?" She picked up one of the towels from the pile on the floor and tossed it to

Melanie. "Is something going on that I should know about?"

Melanie wiped her face and head, and then she got up and started pulling the sheets off the bed. "I am really sorry about this, JoAnne," she said so earnestly that RayBob knew she was having a hard time keeping a straight face.

"There was a little problem," RayBob said. Melanie was tugging the sheet out from under him, so he stood up. He grinned at JoAnne. "There was something in the shower."

Melanie snorted.

"Something in the shower," JoAnne said.

"Remember I told you Chill was spending his time in the bathroom?" RayBob said.

"You said he locked himself in," JoAnne said.

"Yeah, well, that was a joke. But what it was, there was a possum in the shower."

JoAnne looked from RayBob to Melanie and back.

"Really," he said, and he went over and flung open the door. The possum lay where they'd left it, dark and wet on top of the garbage bag.

"The poor little thing," JoAnne said. She went in and bent over to look at it. "It's so tiny." She touched its paw. "It's like a little hand, isn't it? Just like little fingers."

Melanie, clutching the bundle of sheets, looked at RayBob.

"The poor little thing," RayBob said.

"You ever consider a comeback tour?"

"No," RayBob said, tamping down the dirt over the possum's grave. Melanie had departed, JoAnne was comforting Chill, and RayBob, Guido, and Carl were out behind the garage doing men's work. "I never did."

"Think about it," Guido said, handing him back his beer. "You've got a lot of fans out there."

"Naah," RayBob said. "I've lost touch with that stuff. It was a long time ago."

"People change, I guess," Guido said as they headed back toward the house. "You know, when I first met JoAnne I couldn't believe she was your girlfriend. I'd wanted to meet you since I was fourteen years old! And there I was, sl—dating RayBob Van Gelder's ex-girlfriend."

"Sleeping on his used water, too," Carl whispered silently.

RayBob felt strangely exhilarated. He supposed that the shock of the morning had released some hormone or other and now he was drifting along on a natural high, better than drugs, better than drink. Guido wasn't such a bad guy. He had more hair on his upper lip than on top of his head; he didn't wear an earring; and RayBob was pretty sure, even without looking again at the picture stuffed behind JoAnne's jewelry box, that the man in it wasn't Guido at all, but somebody else entirely.

He got his duffel bag from the guest room and carried it out to the front door. "Sorry about the mess," he said.

"Don't be silly," JoAnne said. "I'm just glad you were here for Chill. I think he's sorry to see you go."

They all looked at Chill, who was back in RayBob's old chair. Chill turned his head away.

"He isn't sorry to see *me* go, though," Carl said from the front stoop.

41

"God, what a great voice!" Guido said, slapping RayBob on the back. "JoAnne's told me all about Carl the Human Dog! God, that's great."

RayBob looked at JoAnne. She moved a little closer to Guido and put her arm through his. "So," she said, "you and Melanie are together now?"

"Strictly business," RayBob said. "Come on, Carl." He picked up his bag and went down the steps toward his truck, and when he looked back Guido waved.

Halfway down the block, RayBob glanced in the rearview mirror just in time to see JoAnne pull away from Guido and run down the steps. She was waving both her arms above her head, and she ran out into the street after the truck. He could see her mouth moving, calling, "RayBob! RayBob, come back!"

"Step on it," he said in Carl's voice, and he turned the corner and put a heavy foot on the accelerator.

"Great voice, Carl," he said.

Carl, looking out the back window, snorted. He turned around twice and lay down, stretching his neck so he could rest his big round head on RayBob's thigh. "You ever consider a comeback tour?"

"One problem with that, Carl," RayBob said. "I never have been gone." He whacked Carl on the back, and was pleased at how warm and solid it was, how strongly muscled, and how prickly the short little hairs felt against his palm. He kept his hand there most of the way as they drove on home, laughing as if their lives depended on it.

The Third Person

"I'm trying to decide about an autologous bone marrow transplant," Starr said into the telephone. "Now's the time if I'm ever going to do it."

Starr had been saying this to every Tom, Dick, and Harry for the last two weeks, sounding as if she was trying to decide about a new color scheme for the living room, and Libby was sick to death of it. A stranger or the mailman or a friend they hadn't seen in months would say, "How's it going?" and Starr would say, "I'm trying to decide about a bone marrow transplant." It *trivialized* it, Libby thought. It was like airing dirty laundry.

"If I don't talk about it, it's going to keep getting bigger and scarier," Starr had told her. And of course Libby knew she was right. Libby couldn't talk about it and she was scared to death.

Starr hung up and leaned her head against the back of the sofa. She looked better now than she had looked for a long time. She had a full head of hair and the circles under her eyes were gone and there was color in her cheeks. Libby thought she looked so well that if she hadn't gone back to the doctor for a checkup there would be nothing wrong with her at all.

"I have to decide, Lib," Starr said, turning to look at her.

"Yep," Libby said. She was helpless in this. She could do all the cooking and cleaning and driving, she could hold Starr's head while she threw up, and she could read aloud to her, but she couldn't give advice. If there was any advice to give, she didn't know what it was.

"I'll have to call Choral one of these days," Starr said.

Libby felt her heart contract. "What are you going to tell her?" she said.

Starr shrugged. "I don't know," she said. "Just give her a chance to get used to the idea."

Starr and Libby's daughter, Choral, had married Clay Basin the summer after she graduated from high school and was now the mother of four small girls. With the announcement of each new pregnancy Starr and Libby had gritted their teeth, and when they were alone they let their guard down and looked despondently at each other.

"Where did we go wrong?" Starr said.

Libby shook her head. "You can't convince me we're at fault," she said. "We did the best we could, and now we just have to accept her."

"I know that," Starr snapped. "I just can't understand how she turned out to be so different from us."

"It ain't nature," Libby said, "and it sure ain't nurture."

"We should have been more vigilant," Starr said.

"Oh, come on," Libby said. "She heard plenty of ZPG propaganda growing up."

"Well, it wasn't enough, was it?" Starr said. "There was so much procreation floating around in the media, she breathed it in. It sank its little hooks in her heart and she was a goner."

"Nonsense," Libby said. "*I* think it's a deep cynicism and hopelessness. She feels helpless to make any changes in the world, so she's just enjoying her personal domestic life. It's not unlike what we did."

"The consequences are profoundly different," Starr said. "Our personal life was designed to affect no one but us."

"Our folks weren't very happy about it, as I recall," Libby said.

"They came around, though, didn't they?" Starr said.

"It's a parent's job," Libby said, "to come around."

And of course Starr and Libby had themselves come around. After all, there was no sense in trying to punish Choral or her daughters by withholding affection or financial assistance. The little girls were here; they might as well be enjoyed and indoctrinated. So every month they sent a hefty check off to Germany, where Clay was stationed and Choral was raising children. What else was their money for?

"Our old age," Starr said.

"Honey," Libby said, "we're already grandparents. How much older can we get?"

"At this rate we have a damned good chance of becoming great-grandparents and more," Starr said.

"Wouldn't that be funny?" Libby said, but when she saw

the look Starr gave her, she said, "Oops. Not politically correct."

It wasn't unusual for Libby to feel that she was failing Starr. Over the years, off and on, when their relationship was going through rough times, she had had a fantasy of snatching Choral and running home to her own mother in Cutbank. She had a fierce love for Choral, an overwhelming desire to carry her around and squeeze her pale little toes, and she was filled with endless delight every time Choral turned over, or farted, or screwed up her little red face before crying. She had felt guilty, as if loving Choral so much had meant there was less love left over for Starr.

And secretly she had always believed that Choral loved her a little more than she loved Starr. She thought that perhaps Choral confided more in her than in Starr. Libby was ashamed that this made her happy, but she suspected it was normal for a child to like one parent a little more than the other. It was so difficult to know what was natural and what was the influence of society.

"Isn't society natural?" Choral had once asked during dinner. "I mean, what else is there?"

"In human affairs, choice is always involved," Starr had answered, a little pompously, Libby thought. "The society Libby and I would choose is not the predominant one in our culture."

"Free love," the twelve-year-old Choral had said, rolling her eyes. "That could really mean anything, couldn't it?"

"Exactly," Starr said.

Libby had worked at the public library with Lucretia Basin, Clay's mother, since Clay and Choral were toddlers. Sitting in the same office for twenty years, Libby and Lucretia had become very close. They not only understood each other, each picking up sentences and reference projects where the other dropped them, but they had even grown to look alike. Many a patron had mistaken one plump, beskirted, frizzy-headed figure for the other, until she turned around.

"It's not that I mind Clay marrying white bread," Lucretia had said. "It's that I mind him marrying so young."

"I know exactly what you mean," Libby said. "Some of my best friends are colored, but I never thought my daughter would marry one before she was of age."

They laughed uproariously, but Lucretia was just as tight-lipped as Libby when each new baby came along.

"Boys will be boys," Libby said.

"Oh, Miz Scarlet, I don't know nothin' 'bout no birth control," Lucretia would whine.

They understood each other perfectly.

"Chances are I have half my life still to live," Libby said now as they sat in the staff lounge eating lunch. "I could get a new career. I could start over in a new town with a new identity. I could raise a new family."

"You having a crisis?" Lucretia said, squinting at her over her liverwurst.

"I feel unsettled," Libby said. "Here I am, a grandmother, and I'm still waiting for something to happen."

"Life is what happens," Lucretia said. "Join the Peace Corps."

"That's not it," Libby said. "All the radical things I've done. All the things that seemed so exciting and brave. All that effort we put into raising Choral and she just pops out babies."

Lucretia leaned back in her chair. "Makes me feel better, though. The two of you didn't do any better than I did by my lonesome."

"Maybe it's different for you," Libby said. "Clay was all yours."

"Day in and day out," Lucretia said. "Stop being so hard on yourself, girl."

"I'm the same age as the President of the United States," Libby said. She sighed. "I suppose I'd be disappointed no matter what I'd done."

"I would guess," Lucretia said, looking shrewd, "that Starr isn't doing so well."

Libby made a face. "She's trying to decide about the bone marrow transplant," she said. "And I'm no help at all."

"You're probably wrong about that," Lucretia said. "She'd be lost without you."

"Maybe," Libby said.

"So what did Choral say?" Libby said at dinner.

Starr rolled her eyes. "She started shouting at me. 'My God,' she says, 'you're at the end of a gangplank! Out between the pirates and the deep blue sea! You *gotta* choose!'"

Libby laughed. "That child always had a way with clichés."

"But that wouldn't be any choice at all," Starr said. "I'd take the pirates no question."

"Starr," Libby said, "if you had it to do over, would you do it differently?"

"That's a really stupid question, Libby," Starr said. "What if I said yes?"

"Oh, I don't know," Libby said, drawing a happy face in her lentils with her fork. "Lucretia says I'm having a midlife crisis."

"Right on schedule," Starr said.

"I just feel like I haven't accomplished anything."

"Thanks a lot," Starr said. "I thought our relationship was a success."

"It is," Libby said. "But only for *us*. It doesn't really affect anything else."

"The personal—" Starr said.

"But it *isn't*," Libby said. "At least it isn't political *enough*. We haven't converted anyone, we haven't changed a single institution, and even our daughter has reverted to tradition." She shrugged. "Maybe we took everything too seriously."

"Yeah," Starr said. "As if we only had one chance to get it right." She reached over to pat Libby's hand. "You should get away. There's no reason you have to be here through all of this. Go somewhere else. Do something different."

"Now you're being dumb," Libby said. "I wouldn't leave you."

"Maybe you should," Starr said. "It might be easier for both of us."

"What do you mean?" Libby said.

"Well, sometimes," Starr said, "I worry about you more than I worry about myself."

"Don't," Libby said.

"I can't help it," Starr said, smiling.

That night as she lay in bed Libby imagined herself taking a vacation. Club Med? Outward Bound in the Rockies? Or maybe the Peace Corps, as Lucretia had suggested.

She turned over and peered at the window, where the dark shapes of trees were silhouetted against the slightly lighter sky. When they had first bought this house, Choral was just a little girl, and an owl had lived out in the woods behind them. They had heard it at night, and once, when Libby turned on the porch light before dawn, it had been perched on the bird feeder, turning its head to look for the mice who snuck out in the darkness for the fallen sunflower seeds. But Choral was a grown woman now, and the owl was gone; the woods behind the house had been sold and cut down, and now only a thin fringe of trees separated their house from a tract development. Libby had done nothing to stop it; she had failed to save the owl, and she had failed to save Choral from a pedestrian, unproductive life of barefoot pregnancy.

"There's so much else out there!" she had cried when Choral announced her marriage plans.

And now Libby was on the verge of being out there herself.

Choral called her at the library. "What's this about Mom getting her bone marrow nuked?" she said.

"Well, that's it," Libby said. "Then they put it back and hope for the best."

"It sounds bogus to me," Choral said. "Do you think I should come home?"

"She's fine right now," Libby said.

"Mom," Choral said, "I don't think she's fine if they want

her to get her marrow zapped. I thought maybe I should bring the girls home to say good-bye now, while she seems normal."

Libby felt as if Choral had just sliced her heart in half.

"Mom?" Choral said. "You still there?"

"Did she ask you to come home?" Libby said.

"No," Choral said. "She was crying, mostly. I couldn't understand a lot of what she said."

"Oh," Libby said.

"It's a pain traveling with them," Choral said. "But I think maybe I should."

"I don't know," Libby said. "Let me get back to you."

"Sure, Mom," Choral said, and Libby could picture her exasperated blue eyes. "We'll do lunch."

Libby hung up and sat staring out the tiny window at the roof of the building next door, where dozens of pigeons spent the days hunched up along the eaves, gazing stupidly into space. Why on earth had she gone on about being a failure last night? It was the last thing Starr needed to hear.

"I'm pretty self-centered, aren't I?" she said when Lucretia came back from explaining the Dewey Decimal System to someone out at the reference desk.

"No more than most," Lucretia said. "Why do you ask?"

Libby told her what Choral had said on the phone. "Do you think Starr's made her decision?"

"Not necessarily," Lucretia said. "Could be it's just the other side of things. Her stiff upper lip is as real as her crying about it."

"The other night she said I was making it harder for her," Libby said. "I didn't take it seriously."

"You can only do what you can do," Lucretia said. "The earth is going to spin no matter what."

"How did you get so wise?" Libby said, looking up at her friend.

"Looked it up in a book," Lucretia said. She sat down beside Libby. "You are definitely low in your spirits. Maybe you need to come to Jesus."

"Oh, Lucretia," Libby groaned. "You promised you'd never preach at me."

"I never promised anything of the sort," Lucretia said. "Anyway, to everything there is a season."

Libby hid her face in her hands. "You're wasting your time."

"Just give it a chance," Lucretia said. "No money down, no obligation. *And* an incredible smorgasbord of worship methods for you to select from." She pulled her stool closer to Libby. "I am about as skeptical as they come. All African-American women are about as skeptical as they come. And if *I* believe, *you* can believe. Simple." She sat back, her shoulders slumped and her hands between her knees. "That's all I'm going to say. I am just planting the seed."

"Well, thanks for your concern, Lucretia, but your seed has fallen on barren soil," Libby said.

"That is exactly what I said to Cabin W. Shoe twenty-five years ago," Lucretia said, "and nine months later to the day, little Clay Basin weighed in at eight pounds nine ounces."

Libby laughed. "Is that what's going to happen to me? An immaculate conception?"

"Wasn't so immaculate, as I recall," Lucretia said.

. . .

"I keep thinking the answer will just come to me," Starr was saying into the phone as Libby walked in. She blew Libby a kiss. "You wouldn't believe the gaping holes in my body. I mean, it doesn't look so bad to the naked eye but there's a lot gone."

Libby sighed and took off her coat. She had come home feeling contrite and determined to communicate, and here was Starr babbling on to some outsider again.

"I don't know," Starr said. "I keep waiting for this final stage, right? Acceptance? And it doesn't come. It doesn't seem real." She laughed. "Well, of *course* the chemo was real. I thought I'd puke my guts out. But I didn't want to die, I just wanted to stop puking."

"I can't believe you," Libby said when Starr finally hung up. "You talk as if it's all a big joke."

Starr shrugged. "What do you want me to do, tear my hair?" She patted the top of her head. "Just when it's finally grown back?"

"I don't know," Libby said. She flung herself onto the sofa and pushed her shoes off. "I guess I just feel kind of left out."

"I see," Starr said. "And which aspect of all this did you particularly want to share?"

"Oh, honey, I don't mean that," Libby said. "I just don't want you protecting me all the time."

"Did it ever occur to you that I'm not even thinking about you?" Starr said. "That maybe I'm trying to figure things out myself?"

"Yes," Libby said. "As a matter of fact it did. It just seems like you tell half the world things you don't tell me."

"What do I tell them that you don't already know?" Starr said. "You were *there* when I was puking my guts out."

"That's what I mean," Libby said. "It's kind of a personal thing, between us."

Starr came over and sat down beside her. "I'm not telling people the intimate details."

"Of course not," Libby said. "They'd hang up in disgust." She sighed again. "Lucretia thinks I need religion."

"Well, maybe she's right," Starr said. "Maybe you're ripe for saving."

Libby rolled her eyes. "Betrayed on the home front."

"No, really," Starr said. "You've been moping around about your life. Maybe God's the answer."

"What if I started talking in tongues?" Libby said.

Starr laid her head back against the sofa and smiled at the ceiling. "Debbie Pirkle and I used to take long bubble baths together and talk in tongues the whole time. *Wah-shathebacka! Wah-shamatose!*" She laughed. "Then years later at high school graduation her mother told me her whole family used to stand outside the bathroom door laughing hysterically. I could have died."

"'Bath Babblers Exposed in Beloit,'" Libby said. "What a scandal."

Starr took Libby's hand and held it. "I guess," she said, "I don't really believe a bone marrow transplant would work."

Libby squeezed her eyes shut for a second. "But there's a chance," she said.

"There's a chance without it, too," Starr said. "And what about money?"

"We can cash in our bonds," Libby said. "When you get back to work you can earn it back."

"Libby," Starr said, "it would wipe us out. And chances are that I'd never get back to work. And all your savings would be gone."

"You sound like you're giving up," Libby said.

"I *feel* like I'm being realistic," Starr said. "It's stupid to spend thousands of dollars just so I can be sick for another six months."

Libby shook her head. "You could have a lot of years ahead of you."

"Oh, Lib," Starr said. "We should have known this would happen. When it's us that's involved our principles shoot right out the window."

"That's perfectly normal," Libby said.

"Of course it is," Starr said. "That's why you make rules in advance."

"I don't want to lose you," Libby said.

"Libby," Starr said, leaning toward her, "I'm going to die."

That night Libby couldn't sleep at all. She got up and walked through the house with the lights off, peering at the thousand familiar objects in the moonlight, hoping to see something new. She and Starr had stepped onto a final high platform, a windswept precipice, and she had expected to see a new valley opening up below, but everything was old and familiar and dreary. There was no promised land, just her mother's old eight-day clock in the hall, the Scandinavian rocker that Starr had splurged on two Christmases ago, the eight million books that she and Starr had collected over a lifetime together. Starr's lifetime.

She went into the kitchen and sat down at the table—the old oak table that Starr had refinished. She took the lid off the Waterford sugar bowl that she and Starr had bought in Ireland, and she licked the tip of her finger and pressed it onto the surface of the sugar. When she lifted it it was coated with grains of sugar that all looked the same in the dim light coming through the window, white and tiny and stupid.

"Stupid," Libby said, and she licked the grains off. She sat there eating sugar, plunging her finger into the bowl until it was sore from the rubbing of tiny granules against her skin. She heard her mother's clock strike once in the upstairs hall.

Libby's mother had been dead for ten years, but it still took her by surprise sometimes. I'll have to tell Mom about that, she would find herself thinking when she saw a remarkable sunset, or read a good story, or watched a bird peck at the suet feeder in an entertaining way. It only lasted a split second, this forgetting that her mother was dead, but it was disappointing every time to realize she had no one to call, no one to report to.

Just now she had thought of calling her mother to tell her that Starr was going to die. Her mother, who had not only come around to accepting Starr but had grown to think of her as a second daughter, would have been sad to hear it, and would have said something comforting to Libby.

Now it was Libby who would have to think up something comforting to say to Choral.

• • •

The three women got to the airport early and made their way to the lounge overlooking International Arrivals. They leaned in a row against the glass wall, watching most of the population of the world stream by below. Parents in turbans dragged glossy-haired children past batches of Asian tourists in face masks, and bronzed Germans in fluorescent ski togs elbowed bedraggled Americans out of their way, as everyone inched toward the Customs inspectors.

"Where the hell are all these people going?" Lucretia said.

"God knows," Libby said.

"I always try to imagine which ones are in trouble," Starr said. "Heading for Mexico to get laetrile or something."

"What I can't figure out is where they all get the money to travel," Lucretia said.

"Remember when we went to Ireland? B.C.," Starr said. "Before Choral."

"It seems impossible that anything was before Choral," Libby said. And it did seem, as she thought about it, that her real life had started when Choral was born. The things that had happened to her before that happened to someone else, a person with all the world open to her and all choices available. As soon as Choral came along, everything had narrowed down to Choral and Libby and Starr, and nothing else counted.

And it would change again one of these days. Just as Choral had appeared like a miracle, not here one minute but the center of the universe the next, so Starr would suddenly, despite their years of preparation, be gone. Bing. Just like that. And Libby would be a third person, in a third life.

She looked at Starr, who had closed her eyes and was leaning her forehead against the glass. Last night Libby had worked late, and when she walked in the front door, she had been about to call out when she heard Starr's voice up in the bedroom.

"The pain in my back is getting worse," Starr was saying. "I don't think I could face it if I didn't know that it's going to stop for good pretty soon."

Libby felt a surge of fury. Why hadn't Starr told *her* that the pain was so bad?

"I have to admit it's a relief," Starr said. "It's as if I've totally dropped some huge burden. And now I can get on to the next thing."

Libby stomped across the hall. What was she, a total stranger? Weren't they in this together? She picked up the telephone, but there was no one on the line. All she heard was the dial tone.

She carefully put the phone down and stood for a moment staring into the living room at a painting she and Starr had bought a long time ago. It was a painting of a hilly field in summer, and at one end of the field, at one side of the picture, stood a lone maple tree silhouetted against huge, threatening storm clouds. Even though Starr had grown up in Beloit and Libby in Cutbank, it had reminded both of them of their childhoods.

Libby tiptoed back across the hall. She felt that her heart was broken forever; she heard it creak and felt it silently fall to pieces as she slammed the front door and called, "Hi, honey, I'm home!"

"There they are!" Lucretia shouted, and the three of them

pressed against the glass, peering down at the mass of people below.

And there they were, just coming through the door marked Arrivals, Choral pushing a stroller with two infants in it and a tiny girl clinging to either side. Libby found herself pounding on the glass, and Starr was practically jumping up and down.

"Up here!" Lucretia called, though of course no one on the floor below could hear anything through the thick glass.

But Choral looked up, scanning the rows of people pressed against the windows, and when at last her eyes fell on the three women, she broke into a smile. She knelt down and pointed up at them, and in one motion the little girls turned their faces up toward their grandmothers, except the tiniest one, who kept her eyes on her own mother. And the little girls smiled and began to wave, even the baby, although she was laughing and waving at the beaming Saudi businessman who was playing peekaboo over Choral's shoulder.

Only the oldest of the little girls, who was not very old, would remember much about this visit, and what she would best remember would be this very moment of arrival, when she looked up and saw her three grandmothers way up among a host of people who bobbed near the ceiling, as if big flapping wings were keeping them up, and every one of the bobbing people was smiling down and waving right at her. What she would remember less clearly was a dimly lit living room that smelled a little bit like French toast, and one of the grandmothers holding her on her lap in a rocking chair and reading a story about some frogs, but she could never remember which grandmother it was.

The Rich Man's Easy Charm

In the winter of that year I went to live with my father while my mother sailed around the world with a rich man named Neal. Out of all the people who had answered his personal ad, Neal had picked her. He said I could come, too, if I knew how to sail, but my mother looked at me and shook her head. "Christy's got school," she said. "Seventh grade's an important year."

I shrugged and smiled at Neal, and I took my books down to the island.

"Bon voyage," my father said to my mother when she dropped me off. He stood on the porch of the cabin, scratching Wretch's head, as I followed her up the path to the car.

"You'll be fine," my mother said to me. She hugged me and squeezed my face against her shirt for a long time. "You like your dad. You'll get along."

"It's not like he's a stranger," I said. "I've known him all my life."

She held me away from her and looked at my face. "Even if he was," she said, "people don't stay strangers very long. You get

61

to know someone pretty fast when you're living with him."

"Bon voyage," I said.

"Don't be a fresh kid," she said. "And do what he tells you."

"Wacko," my father said. He'd carried a box of my books into the house and was sitting on my bed, watching me unpack my suitcase. "She's crazy."

"She just gets along with people really well," I said. Wretch had lain down in the middle of the floor and I had to step over him each time I put something in a drawer. "She's very outgoing."

"You're right," my father said. "A year on a yacht with a stranger is nothing to her."

"He won't be a stranger for long," I said. I looked at my father and we both laughed.

I was tired of the whole thing. My mother's optimism wore me down, and I was relieved to be with my father, who had a glum view of the world and didn't believe anything would improve the situation.

Wretch had been following me around since I arrived, gloomily watching me unpack, halfheartedly going into the bathroom with me. "You got yourself a buddy," my father said when he noticed it.

"He feels I'm his responsibility," I said, watching Wretch scratch an ear with a hind foot. "I'm a burden on him."

"It's good for him," my father said. "He's been leading the life of Riley since you left."

"He doesn't like change," I told him. "Poor old thing, he wants everything to be the same as it used to be."

"The sign of a true dog," my father said. He was always pointing at the white spot on Wretch's forehead and telling him, "That's where we'll aim when you get feeble." Wretch would just stare off in another direction and slowly let his eyes close. That's how much he cared.

I got a card from my mother right away, one she had mailed from town before she even got off the island, but it only said that she loved me very much, I was still her little girl, and she would be thinking of me every minute. It clued me in that I hadn't convinced her that her going on this trip was fine with me, that I wanted her to be happy and I thought this might be just the thing. I hadn't even cried when she said good-bye, because I knew she was prone to guilt. Now I saw that that had been a tactical error.

But when a long time passed and I didn't get any more cards, I guessed that once she'd gotten together with Neal—the rich man—she'd gotten happier. I hoped it lasted.

The island was a true island, but it was attached to the mainland by a bridge. You could have walked to the mainland at low tide if the rocks hadn't been so slippery. My mother and I had moved away a couple of years before, when I was still quite young, and had lived ever since in a house she rented from a professor at the U. Every morning she waited with me for the school bus, and when I got on she waved and got into the car and drove off to the U. She was working on a degree in communications. I thought it was a good field for her.

When we first moved away I had thought that my life was ending. I had always lived on the island, and I had never lived without my father, and I thought that leaving them meant that I would become someone else. But now that I was back, I was neither my old self nor a new person; I was like someone caught between universes, or a character waiting nowhere while a page of the story was being turned.

After we'd left, my father built a cabin down on the back side of the island. It had two bedrooms, his and mine, and the wall between our rooms was thin enough for me to hear him snoring. We had no close neighbors but we lived at the end of a road strung with houses and trailers, and everyone who lived in them knew my father and me. The school bus stopped at the bottom of that road and I would walk up it every evening, hoping no one would be out in the yard. Sometimes little children would be playing outside one of the trailers and would stare at me, and outside another one a very fat man sometimes sat in his garden, poking at weeds with his cane. Smoke came out the chimneys of the houses and trailers as I passed.

When I got to the last curve in the road, Wretch would be there, lying like a sphinx at the very corner of my father's property, and when he saw me he would get to his feet and wag his tail slowly, as if it were very heavy, and walk over and sniff at me. Then we would go up the drive to the house.

My father was a game warden, and at certain times of the year he went out in the woods with the other wardens and sat up all night in stakeouts. When I had trouble sleeping I pictured him out looking for poachers, driving along the back roads under the trees, rolling into little turnouts and shutting off the engine and the lights and just sitting there in the woods waiting for men to break the law. I found this a comforting vision, and after a while I could slip off to sleep, Wretch snoring on the rug beside me.

My father was fair but he was a stickler for the rules. The spring before I came back he had broken up a poaching ring that had been going on for years and was the major livelihood of half a dozen men on the island, including Win Salsbury, who lived in one of the trailers on our road.

"The law," Win Salsbury said in a loud voice one time when we walked into Betty's Kitchen for breakfast.

The men at his table got quiet but my father said, "The law is the law is the law," and waved at them as we walked on by to our regular table. I looked at Win Salsbury while we waited for Betty to take our order and he was just talking to the other men as if he didn't care, but when they left he nodded at my father.

"Have a nice day, parson," he said.

My father waved again and when they were gone he leaned across his coffee and said to me, "I believe he *meant* that, Christy."

"Why did he call you parson?" I said.

"He thinks I am a shepherd of men," my father said, "and he was trying to get my goat."

The poachers were found guilty, but they all received suspended sentences. My father was angrier than I had ever seen him. "Goddamn right I take it personally," he shouted at someone from his office over the phone. "I might as well be out loading their guns for them. I might as well take up taxidermy and make some money."

He hung up and slammed himself into a chair at the table where I sat silently staring at my homework. "Jesus," he said, drumming his fingers on the table. "Two years of work down the drain. I think there is no justice in this world, Christine. Wretch," he said, looking down at him where he lay asleep on the rug, "you are the only one in the family whose misery we can put you out of. The rest of us must suffer through to the end."

"Legally, anyway," I said. "What's a suspended sentence?"

"A suspended sentence is—" He sat for a moment with his mouth open, and then he grinned. "Just that. A sentence in which nothing happens at all."

I didn't know how long I would be living with my father. Neal's ad for crew for his boat had said a year or around the world, whichever came first. When my mother read it she snorted and said, "I'll take him around the world." The paper was a weekly which came on Wednesdays and my mother bought it mainly for the personal ads.

"Even if it takes more than a year?" I said, looking up from my math homework.

"Won't take that long," she said. She circled the sailor's ad with her red Flair. She read the next one aloud. "'Walking on the beach, champagne at sunrise, intelligent, sensitive, liberal. Children okay.' Hear that, Christy?"

"Generous of him," I said. I could listen to my mother with one ear while I did my math. Math was easy for me.

"The sailor doesn't say anything about children on this cruise," she said. "I'll try him anyway, just for kicks."

And of course Neal *did* say children were okay. "Think how much she'd learn," he said to my mother.

"Christy doesn't like sailing," my mother said. "She's a landlubber. Just like her dad."

My mother loved sailing more than she loved almost anything else, but my father got seasick at the drop of a hat, and although she gave a hundred other reasons for leaving my father and moving up to the U, I secretly believed that the real reason was their incompatibility over the sea. I believed it was a general truth about human relations: sailors and landlubbers are oceans apart.

I hated sailing, I always got seasick, and I was always, always cold on a boat, even in midsummer. I was shy and quiet and a loner, and I could accept these things, but I would have given anything to like sailing. But I knew I would always be like my father in this. Those winter mornings when I looked out the window of the school bus at the sea smoke rising out of the harbor, I felt as if it was rising up in me, filling my stomach and my lungs and my head and obscuring my life. I was in limbo, trying to love the ocean and hating myself because I never would.

"Have you heard anything more from your mother?" my father asked one Saturday morning as we ate breakfast at Betty's.

"Nope," I said. I could feel him trying to think of something comforting to say, so I looked up at him. "They had a lot of provisioning to do."

For a second his eyebrows popped up from behind his glasses and then they dropped down again. "At least another card," he said.

I shrugged. "So she's irresponsible. She'll write when she gets time."

"Christy," my father said, "is there anything you want? Is there something I'm overlooking?"

"No," I said. "Wretch sees to it that I'm comfortable."

"Because if I am, you have only to say the word." He watched me finish my cereal. "And the word is fetch. Just say, 'Fetch, Wretch,' and the world is yours."

"He never fetched anything in his life," I said.

"No," my father said.

It was January, the dead of winter, and while the number of daylight hours was increasing, the days were still very short. I never saw my father in daylight during the week, so that each Saturday when we finished breakfast and walked out of Betty's into the parking lot and the morning light hit him in the face, I was always startled. Every time he was a different person. He looked old, or he looked unshaven, or, most shocking of all, he had a pimple on his chin. I was starting to get pimples, and I was sensitive to them. I was never ready for what I saw, and I felt as if I was shaking my head and stomping my feet, snorting like a horse in the cold, trying to shake the collected sea smoke out of myself and see my father clearly.

He made fun of the personals in the weekly paper. "'SWF seeks tall, advanced degree SWM who looks at life with an unclouded eye.' What do you think, Christy?"

"An unclouded eye?" I said, not paying a lot of attention, because math was harder at the island school.

"That's what the lady says," my father said. "Here's one.

'Sensuous, *zaftig* SWF seeks accepting, caring M for gourmet dining, movies, family.'"

"Is *zaftig* something to do with sex?" I said.

"Fat," my father said. "A fat lady who wants to get married." He sighed. "Probably I should date. I have grieved for your mother long enough."

I was surprised, but I just said, "I should think so."

He waved the newspaper back and forth in front of him. "I don't believe, though, that this is the way to go about it. There is something absolutely wrong about this."

"I think," I said carefully, "you have to be a certain kind of person to do that. It's okay for some people."

My father was quiet, and I went back to my homework. I listened to my pencil scrape across the scratch paper and to my father, who was breathing deeply through his nose, which whistled just a little with each exhalation.

"It's hard to live without doing harm," my father finally said. "The worst harm we do is to our children. And yet"—his voice grew jocular—"who is to say? Why should we be any different from the rest of the animal kingdom? Who has the gall to blame us?"

I shook my head and wrote figures on my paper, pretending to be absorbed in mathematics.

"Wretch!" my father said. "At least with you we'll know exactly where to aim."

Wretch's feet twitched ever so slightly.

"He's deep in dreamland," I said.

"Aren't we all," my father said.

For a while my mother had dated the professor who owned our house, and a couple of men she met in classes, but she wasn't like the mothers you read about who go crazy about boyfriends after they get divorced. She said she was more interested right now in getting her degree and making something of her life. But when I saw her with Neal the rich man, I realized that she just had different standards than most women around. Neal was tall and thin like my father, but he smiled a lot and was comfortable talking to me.

"He is a rich man, isn't he?" my mother said the day after she'd been out on her first date with him.

"What do you mean?" I said.

"The rich man's easy charm," my mother said. "You liked him, didn't you?"

"He was okay," I said.

She puffed out her cheeks at me. "Well, he liked you," she said. "He's the sort of man who gets along with anybody."

And I supposed that was it. Neal would get along with anyone. He took people as they came. But my father was more reserved.

"You can judge a man by his dog," my mother had said once. "Always get to know the dog, Christy."

"Right," my father said. It was dinnertime. "If a dog bites, the man will bite."

"If the dog pays no attention to you, you can bet the man will forget you once the party's over," my mother said, looking down at her plate and picking up beans on the tines of her fork. "You can bet the man has far more important things to think about."

"Wretch doesn't pay much attention to anyone," I said, "but Daddy pays a lot of attention to us."

They were both silent for a long moment and then my mother said, "Why, I hadn't even noticed that."

Trying to rectify what I'd done, I forced a giggle and said, "Then it's *you* that doesn't pay attention."

But the resulting silence was so dangerous that I had to clutch the edge of the table. When such things happened we were all at a loss as to what to do next; but I felt that my parents were simply puzzled, oblivious to my danger, while I knew that at any second I might be demolished by what had been released and now ricocheted around the room. It didn't happen often. I was too careful.

I had never felt unloved. I was glad that my mother had found a rich man. I imagined her after she dropped me off, driving back to our rented house, stopping to mail my postcard on the way, and flying the next day to Miami to meet Neal. Once in Miami, I knew, they planned to provision the boat and get to know each other well enough to set sail. I wondered how strongly I would figure in the story she would tell about her life. I thought that if anyone had asked *me*, I probably wouldn't have talked too much about *her*, not in my own story. So I figured she'd just mention me in passing. I was a given, since Neal had known about me from the start.

"Understood," Neal would say, nodding a little impatiently, if my mother mentioned my name. "Understood."

• • •

All the waterfront property on that part of the island belonged to rich people who came for the summer. In July and August the woods echoed with the sounds of the summer people, their car engines, the halyards on their sloops, the barks of their springer spaniels, and the voices of their children as they dragged the canoes out of the boathouse. But in the winter the floating docks were hauled out of the water onto the shore and the huge uninsulated cottages sat cold and empty, and I would wade down there through snow that was sometimes thigh-deep.

Unless I came right after a snowstorm, the snow around the cottages was not pristine, because Win Salsbury and the other men on our road had jobs as winter caretakers for the rich people. They drove down on ATV's to check on things. If they saw me they would wave, and I would have to wave back. But they were so noisy I could hear them from far away and step into the woods in time to avoid them. I followed the silence to the empty houses, walking in the ATV tracks through the snow.

This day there was enough silence to hear the juncos and kinglets whispering in the cedars, and down on the water, which was an inlet from the bay, some buffleheads drifted in their insulating feathers. The receding tide had left a thin layer of ice on the rocks, and I crunched down to the very edge of the sea, the ice breaking under my boots, and stood in the wind watching the ducks move effortlessly out of reach.

I made my way back to an empty summer place and, hanging on to the railings, climbed carefully up the snowy steps to the porch. I walked along it, looking out at the sparkling sharp view from the porch, and then peered in a window at the cavernous cold living room. It was a beautiful, frightening room, with one or two pieces of upholstered furniture draped with sheets and the rest, made of birch logs and slatted pine, sitting there bare and waiting for warm weather. All the summer cottages were houses with no heat and no way to get heated, only wide fireplaces that would be next to useless in the cold of winter. I walked on and looked through a bedroom window at the built-in bunks and imagined the children who came there for their vacations, how they loved the smell of cedar and the dampness of the summer wind. There were shelves full of rocks and driftwood, lobster buoys and glass smoothed by the sea. I knew that children treasure such things, and love things that are familiar. I knew how, after they ran in to look at their bunks and their treasures, they would run out onto the porch with the dog barking happily behind them, and find the abandoned Frisbee and throw it toward the sea for the dog to chase.

But except for the sound of a distant chainsaw, it was silent as I stood there. My mother was sailing in southern climes, wearing shorts, floating toward pink beaches where birds I had never heard of nested in the sand, but if she married Neal, the rich man, maybe he would buy one of these summer cottages, and then when I looked in the windows I would be seeing my own mother's life.

"Another world, ain't it," someone said, and I jumped a foot. "Whoa there," he said, and I saw Win Salsbury standing in my tracks at the edge of the porch, grinning at me. "Didn't mean to scare you."

"I didn't hear your vehicle," I said, but I felt as if I could hardly speak, my heart was thumping so hard.

"Damn thing's on the blink," he said. "Walked down."

"Is this your place?" I said. "I mean, do you caretake here?"

He came up on the porch and over to the window, stopping a couple of feet away from me. "If this was my place," he said, "I would not be freezing my ass off on the outside looking in. Sure, I keep an eye on it." I felt him looking at me. "Looks like you do, too."

"I just look," I said. "I don't go in or anything."

"Hey, it's okay with me," he said, lifting his hands. "Us folks in the working class got to stick together."

We both stared hard through the glass.

"You're the warden's kid, aren't you?" he said.

I thought wildly of denying it, but after a second I nodded.

"Well," Win Salsbury said, turning a little toward me, "you must be some proud of him."

I shrugged.

He walked over to the porch railing and stood looking at the gray water. "What do you think of the outcome then?" he said. "Guilty as charged."

"But you got a suspended sentence," I said.

"Right," he said. "And so I got to watch my step, and report in, and never take a deep breath without permission."

I wished I had brought Wretch down with me.

"Your daddy ever teach you to hunt?" Win Salsbury said.

"He doesn't like hunting," I said.

Win Salsbury laughed out loud, a sharp and angry bark. "Don't you believe it," he said. But then he looked at me, and I suppose I looked scared, because he said, "Hell, I like your dad. If he hadn't of got me, I'd like him even better." He smiled at me, and I saw that he was younger than I'd thought, and clean-shaved.

"How can you kill animals?" I said. "I don't know how anyone could do it."

He grunted and looked out at the bay again. "How old are you?" he said.

"Twelve," I said.

"Twelve," Win Salsbury said. "Well, my father taught me to hunt when I was eight years old. I been a hunter for most of my life." He looked at me. "I'm going to tell you something that I have never told anyone. You heard people say that? 'I never told this to anyone before.'" He laughed. "Believe me, it's always a lie. What's your name?"

I told him.

"Christy. Well, Christy," he said, crossing his arms and leaning forward against the railing, "one day, when I was fifteen, me and my cousin Buddy was out hunting. No, we was out shooting. When you're fifteen, you like to shoot. The sound of it grabs you right there—" He jerked his hips against the railing. "Beats hanging out on street corners. So me and Buddy went up along Sheep Creek, you know where that is? Shooting at things, birds and little squirrels and such, just having a time on a cold November gray day. Right?"

I nodded, but he wasn't looking at me.

"We're walking along the creek and it's dismal, the way November is, no color, and Buddy grabs my arm and says, 'Look there!' And I did, and there was something by the water, kind of hunched over beside a stump. We thought it was a huge bird, like a heron. And Buddy lets go of my arm and we both raise up our guns and shoot, just like that. Bang. And the thing slumps over.

"And I got a terrible, terrible feeling right here." He looked at me and thumped his chest with his gloved fist. "Even now I remember exactly how it felt. A black thick pain, right over my heart. And we walked down through the brush, along the water, and when we got up to it—" He waited a minute, staring out at the bay. "When we reached it we saw it wasn't no bird. It was a man, a man in a green coat, and he was dead."

I felt my mouth open, and a chunk of cold air slipped down my throat and stuck there.

"But you know what, Christy?" Win Salsbury looked at me again, his eyes narrow in his cold red face. "When I looked down and saw that man laying there beside the creek, all slumped over and his eyes staring at nothing, and not the big slim feathery bird I'd been expecting, that pain just eased right up out of my chest." He watched my face closely. "Christy, I was *glad* it wasn't no bird. I was glad."

He kept staring at me, as if he was waiting for something, and finally I said, "Did you go to jail?"

He sighed. "Juvies," he said. "Both of us. Underage and accidental. Probation and hunter ed. And then—" He waved his hand in the air. "Clean slate. Square one."

He walked back across the porch and stood looking into the cold empty living room. "Who would ever want to live this kind of life, Christy? Who would want to?"

. . .

That afternoon my father and I went for a long drive on the back roads all over the island, and we ate supper at Betty's Kitchen. The winter was so cold that the strait between the island and the mainland had frozen solid, and on the way home we stopped to look at it. The moon was nearly full and halfway up the sky when we got out of the car and walked down to the foot of the bridge, and the ice was dappled with black moon shadows behind all the rough spots. There was no wind, and the tide was coming in, soft thin waves slipping over the top of the ice and freezing before they could get away.

"Look at that," my father said. "No one admits it was the dead of winter when Christ walked on water."

"It would certainly make it easier to believe," I said.

He laughed.

"I wonder if this ever happened before," I said.

"Not in your lifetime," my father said. We stared at the moonlight on the ice for a minute. "You know, your mother loves you very much."

"Understood," I said.

"What's that supposed to mean?" my father said, genuinely interested. "Is that from school?"

"It's a given," I said.

"Christy," my father said, "*I* love you very much. That's a given."

"People don't understand your humor," I said. "They don't understand that when you talk to Wretch like that you're only joking."

"I don't think anyone else hears me," my father said. "I keep it inside the family."

"It's not just Wretch," I said. "It's the *zaftig* lady, too. Nobody understands."

"Christy," my father said at last, "honey, you don't have to take care of me. I'm the adult."

"I'm taking care of myself," I said.

He shook his head. "That's not right either," he said, "but I don't imagine there's anything I can do about it."

I took a deep breath of icy air and said, "Sometimes I feel like I'm in the middle of a suspended sentence."

My father's laugh shot out over the frozen water and echoed back at us, a sharp *Hah! hah! hah!* that caused something in the trees behind us to take wing. "On the contrary," he said, hugging me too hard, "you are in chapter one."

"Do you think she's irresponsible?" I said.

He held me for a moment and then let me loose. "She's taking care of herself. Which is pretty goddamned responsible. And hard to do."

I stood waiting for something to happen in the dark. I thought the full moon, and the island getting connected to the mainland, and the coldest winter in my life had all come together to indicate something momentous. There was no sound but the thin shooshing of waves on ice, and now and then a car passing over the bridge. A huge sharp feeling of excitement suddenly fluttered up in my chest, and I thought that something must happen soon, and that after all there was a chance that I would be happy in life.

When we got home there would be a postcard from my mother in the mailbox, and the picture on the front would be a brilliant blue-green ocean and a white beach. While my father got the fire going in the woodstove, I would take Wretch outside and stand on the back steps watching his dark shape nose around the yard, his white spot gleaming now and then in the moonlight. Still cold from standing at the edge of the water with my father, I would wait in the dark, rubbing the shiny side of the postcard with my numb fingers, and try to imagine what my mother could possibly have to say.

Everything Is Nothing But
A Learning Experience

"Timmy was an angel," my mother used to say. "A little cherub, sent to earth to bring us joy."

These days, of course, angels are rampant. They crop up onstage and in movies, in fiction both juvenile and adult. There are cherubim on bedspreads, seraphim on rugs and kites and tablecloths. One of my mother's last purchases was a shower curtain, hanging in her shower even now, on which a thoughtful cherub conjugates the verb *lavare*.

There's supposed to be a meaning in this onslaught of celestial beings, something to do with an upsurge in religious beliefs, or an increasing desire for help from high places; but I think there's no more meaning in the rise of angels than in the popping of corn. I believe that angels are invented to fulfill certain needs, and usually those needs are the failures of the people who find it necessary to invent them.

The fact of the matter is that Timmy was born with multiple congenital heart defects, and, as I recall, in his brief span he caused my mother no end of anguish. Not to mention myself and my older brother, Mac, two intelligent, beautiful children who were shunted aside for the nearly three years that Timmy ruled the roost. And not to mention my father, who left.

My mother was greatly disappointed that Mac and I remained barren. She never ceased muttering about it, and as the years went on she became more and more liberal, even libertine, in her desire for grandchildren. "Don't you have a nice lesbian friend," she'd say to Mac, "who would be willing to bear your child?"

"Mother," Mac would say, "I do not want anyone to bear my child, least of all one of my friends."

So she'd aim her little darts in my direction. "Nora, dear," she said, "sometimes I look at you and I can almost hear your clock ticking."

Of course, it was her own clock she heard, and finally *bing!* the alarm rang and she joined Timmy in the clouds. Sometimes when Mac and I are together we look up at the sky and wave. Sometimes I do it when I'm alone.

I went home for my mother's final illness, and I lived in that house on that street in that town for several months, cooking up a lot of broth, though I had a nurse come in to bathe her and all that. After a while my mother said, "Enough of this shit," and stopped eating, and I called Mac. He came home, too, and the next day Mom lapsed into a coma and only came out, presumably, on the other side.

People poured out of the woodwork, every one of them bearing banana bread. When they left Mac and I would cut into yet another loaf and gag, clutching our throats, collapsing on the floor in banana-bread-poisoning agonies, and then we would laugh helplessly for many long minutes, until we lay spent and weeping.

"I didn't think she had so many friends," I said, sitting up with the knife in my hand.

"I've seen it many times," Mac said from the middle of the kitchen floor, and I knew, despite his light tone, that he had. "If you want to know who your real friends are, die."

The day after the funeral he flew back to San Francisco, and I was left to sever our ties. I gave everything away: my mother's good china, my father's Navy uniform, Mac's erector set, Timmy's blankie.

"You're an angel of mercy!" cried the man who sits in the Goodwill truck in the Kroger's parking lot, waiting for castoffs; and I ducked out, not even taking a receipt for tax purposes.

It was the next morning that I stepped out the front door of the empty house and picked up the morning paper to read that the Klan was planning a rally downtown.

"We're putting on all our off-duty men on that day," the chief of police was quoted as saying, "and beforehand we're going to be picking up all those rocks at the base of the trees on Main Street. We don't want any trouble."

I pictured the police force, with the help of the fire department and some of the Elks, earnestly collecting the decorative rocks the merchants had bought several years before to beautify the downtown. Honestly, though, what else could they do? Ban the Klan?

Counterdemonstrations were being planned, as they always are. Ministers of the gospel would be ganging up with the eleven local practitioners of the Jewish faith to combat hatred, and no doubt the town's contingent of African-Americans would join them. There would be speeches by the mayor, songs and prayers, and rides and balloons for the kids. The Klan would take the courthouse steps; the forces of tolerance would be out at the mall.

"Far out," Mac said when I called him. "A love-in."

"Love-ins are dead and gone," I said, "but the Klan marches on."

"I thought they banned the Klan nine hundred years ago," he said.

"Nobody ever told the Klan about it," I said. "They've been biding their time."

"I don't think they're smart enough to bide time," he said. "Who are they, anyway?"

"Outside agitators," I said, and he laughed.

Mac and I had never marched against the Klan, but we once skipped school to go to a rock concert against the war. When we got back we were suspended for three days, and the war continued as if nothing had happened.

I poured myself another cup of coffee and stepped outside again. It would be hot before the day ended, and the air hung heavy with sweet fragrances. I stood on the porch, the hot mug in my hand. Everything smelled good, I was alone, and the world was my oyster.

. . .

It was not long after that day that I looked into the mirror and saw that the left side of my face had fallen. I turned sideways and peered from the corner of my eye at my cheek, poking at it. The little dent left by my finger lingered an iota too long before the flesh pooled back in and drooped earthward again. My skin was no longer elastic. I turned to face myself and squinted, and sure enough, the left jowl hung infinitesimally lower than the right.

"Don't worry," I said, patting the right cheek kindly, "you'll catch up."

I was not, in fact, terribly upset about it. Those of my generational cohort who are still alive are sliding without hiatus toward the millennium; who am I to stall?

"You've got to get out of there," Mac said when I called him.

"It's just a town now, Mac," I said. "Now that Mom's gone, it's just a town."

"It's a black hole," he said. "You may never be heard from again."

"The spring beauties are blooming," I told him. "Remember the spring beauties?"

"Of course I do," he said. "They have nothing to do with anything, Nora. Don't lose touch."

Mac had, as usual, put his finger right on the button. I was finding it hard to leave town. Even without most of the furniture and accumulated dust of fifty years, my mother's house felt more like home than any home I'd had since I left. The black rotary-dial telephone still stood on the same telephone stand at the foot of the stairs, with the phone number of my childhood preserved under the yellowed plastic disc. It was once I had the phone disconnected that I'd be out of touch.

We weren't really shunted aside, Mac and I. We were included in everything. We were told from the start what was wrong with little Timmy, and shown pictures of the human heart, with penciled-in arrows indicating why Timmy's didn't work right. We went with Timmy and my parents to the doctor, and we tried to make him smile while the doctors poked and prodded his tender flesh. We knew from the beginning that he would die young.

"He could go at any time," the grown-ups told us.

We lugged surgical textbooks to school and stood in front of our classes holding them open to photographs gleaming with red flesh and shiny yellow lumps of fat, which we told our classmates were scenes from an open heart. If our teachers complained, our parents defended us: it was our way of handling it.

We loved Timmy, but for years Mac and I longed for a beagle, whom we would have named Happy.

The fact of the matter is that, unbeknownst to my mother, I had tried for years to get pregnant, until at last my husband left me.

"I can't bear it any longer," he'd said from a phone booth in Phoenix. I could hardly hear him over the noise of the desert city.

"How do you think I feel?" I said.

"You keep saying it doesn't really matter if we have any children or not," he said. "But I want children so much it hurts."

"Where?" I said.

"In my heart," he said. "You can have everything. I'll be on the road."

I sat by the phone for a long time, waiting for him to call again, but he didn't. He was right. I hadn't much cared, really, about having children. Probably I had not tried very hard to conceive.

I myself had once driven south out of Phoenix on the long two-lane highway that runs toward the border. Just before dawn I pulled over onto the shoulder and got out to stretch my legs. A carpet of birdsong covered the dark desert floor, and a thin rim of light showed at the horizon.

I hoped my husband would not have that experience.

I went back once more to the cemetery where Mac and I had left the remains of our mother. Her name was fading fast on the temporary cardboard placard. Beside it, the white stone cherub kneeling at Timmy's head had lost his nose, and a delinquent's spray-painted comment had been impossible to completely efface when Mac and I discovered it the day before our mother's funeral. Still it was peaceful there, out at what thirty-five years ago had been the edge of town. The grass was nicely mown, they tried to keep dogs out, the snowball and beauty bushes were in high spirits.

Our father did not leave until after Timmy had died and we had all watched the tiny white box disappear into the ground. There was no stopping the flood of tears. My father wept, my mother wept, the men who bore the coffin wept, all of my parents' friends were weeping. Mac and I stood together beside our weeping parents and cried our young hearts into the grave with our baby brother. No one understood him as well as we did when he asked for water, or for his blankie, or for a good night kiss. He had loved us enormously, and raised his little arms toward us when we entered his room.

Our father left not long after the funeral, though I don't remember him going; he just disappeared from my memories. There had been five of us and then there were three. He never came to see us, never took us to the park on Sundays.

Later he would say it was because, having lost one, he couldn't bear to see the two of us and not keep us, but I think it took him a long time to dream that one up.

The day dawned cloudless and already warm, and I determined to walk to the Klan rally through the streets of my old hometown. There is a certain joy in revisiting the scenes of childhood, and a certain horror as well. Here was where I threw up after riding the Tilt-a-Whirl at the Jaycee Barbecue; here was the alley where a friend was raped; here at the end of the block was the house where, each night after supper, a man shot arrows at the starlings that roosted in the maples.

I peered into store windows, hoping no one would recognize me. The stores had been brightened and plasticized, and the racks of cotton dresses that smelled of sizing had been replaced by baggy organic cotton sweatpants in natural colors. The store where escaped parakeets dwelt in the ceiling fans was gone, and in its place was a thing I had never expected to see on the streets of that town, a high-rise parking lot. Pigeons nested on the roof, and when I walked by their shit crackled underfoot.

As I approached the center of town I was joined by other residents who had chosen to see the Klan in action and were plodding along in twos and threes and small herds. A Head Start class passed in a long line, two by two, each child tied to a rope held by a teacher in front and a mother who brought up the rear. A clown rode by on a unicycle. A pack of Cub Scouts marched along in full blue uniform singing, "Flintstones! Meet the Flintstones!" A vast tour bus loaded with Elderhostelers pulled up at the corner of Main and Washington, and when the door opened the elders descended, slowly and carefully, clinging for dear life to the dark hand of the bus driver who stood at the foot of the steps. Once down they unfolded their walkers, adjusted their hearing aids, and set off with the rest of the crowd for the courthouse square, leaving the driver to lean protectively against the bus and have a smoke.

On Main Street I saw that the decorative stones were indeed gone, and the sorry trees looked naked and vulnerable in their little squares of dirt, countless deserted ant colonies and pale tufts of grass exposed among their pathetic roots. Where once the streets of my youth had been openly traveled by family station wagons, now they were blocked by fire engines and bulldozers, and men in blue stood like hefty guardian angels in front of the Civil War monument. A squad car lurked in every alley, a sharpshooter lay doggo on every other roof.

At the courthouse, a phalanx of black-booted, big-tummied Klansmen, bearing Confederate flags and round shields covered with strange runes, had ranged themselves along the steps.

"I thought they'd be wearing sheets," muttered a skinhead.

"For God's sake, Vern, who'd go out in public wearing a sheet?" his buddy said.

"We shoulda gone to the show at the mall," Vern said.

"You'll be glad you came to this," an Elderhosteler in a Chinese coolie hat said, turning around. "This is history."

"Hell," Vern said, "everything is nothing but a learning experience anyway."

A man on the steps shouted, "Heil!" and the arms of the Klansmen shot violently in the direction of the new high-rise parking lot as another man, in a black shirt that was buttoned up to his Adam's apple, stepped out the door of the courthouse and began to speak.

Weariness assailed me. Try as I might, I could only catch a word here, a word there. I'd never been to a Klan rally before, but somehow it was all familiar—the shouting, the slavering, the calling of names. My eyes closed, and I leaned against the sweaty arm of the woman beside me and felt her slump on me in turn. The sun poured over us and the smell of the crowd rose around us, the smell of suntan oil and perspiration, the smell of a grape sucker in the mouth of a soiled child, the smell of hot tar in the sun where they'd patched the streets in preparation for the rally. The man in the black shirt shouted and the crowd swayed, calmed by the familiar sound, and some hummed along as if they knew the tune quite well but couldn't recall the words.

When Blackshirt shouted something about pure blood, I thought of Happy the Beagle that Mac and I had never had.

When he screamed that Negroes did nothing but breed, I

thought of my husband, somewhere in Arizona.

When he cried out that the unfit would be eliminated, and that AIDS was God's way of punishing the deviant, I heard a sound like thunder, and I opened my eyes.

Above and beyond the Klansmen, behind the courthouse, one of those fancy flying squadrons that taxpayers are so fond of was roaring about the sky in tight formation. They were out at the mall, of course, part of the counterdemonstration. They'd been given strict orders to stay out of the Klan's airspace, but we could see them, and now and then we couldn't help applauding some loop-de-loop, which the Klansmen thought was applause for them, though they never smiled. They stood as motionless as plastic action figures for the whole time.

Finally Blackshirt, too, stood silent, his sweat dripping onto the courthouse steps, and a man of God came out a side door. He patted Blackshirt kindly on the back, wiped his hand on the seat of his pants, and turned to face the crowd.

"Oh, God," he said loudly, and automatically, because of his morose tone, many in the crowd bowed their heads. "Oh Lord, who has seen fit to make many and separate the races of men—"

Beside me, Vern shouted, "Look!"

We all looked up, and there, as if the noise and violence and exhaust of the tricky planes had somehow disturbed the universe, was a veritable rainbow of winged creatures in the distant sky. The colors in their wings gleamed in the sunlight, iridescent azures and magentas, unearthly chartreuses and heliotropes, and as we stared they grew larger, drifting softly toward the face of the earth.

"Jesus is Lord!" someone cried, and a Catholic person in front of me sank to her knees and crossed herself. And then many others fell to their knees, including the silenced Klansman of God, who knelt with difficulty on the steps and raised his arms toward this bright celestial host.

Once more the planes roared by, and in their wake the drifting creatures billowed earthward, dropping toward the distant mall. As I squinted into the bright sky, I saw that the brilliant turquoise wings of one had been caught by a merry little breeze that was bearing it away from its fellows, right in my direction. It coasted this way, and that way, eddied about by the pulsing thermals of our hot planet, and, as I watched open-mouthed, I saw it laugh, and an angelic peal of laughter tinkled down over the crowd, sprinkling my upturned face and delicately touching my tongue like the sweetest of holy waters.

"*Lavo!*" I called, and it may have been my admittedly needy imagination, but I thought I heard the answering cry of a host of voices, "*Lavamus!*"

And the lost angel floated down over the courthouse, caught an updraft from the sun-drenched front steps, and bypassed the upraised arms of the Klansman of God to drop, a little bundle of joy, into my own.

"It was the Family Fun Chute," I said to Mac when I called him.

"The what?" he said.

I spelled it out for him. "Part of the counterdemonstration," I said. "There were whole families bailing out, floating around in the sky. The mayor thought it up."

"Good God," Mac said.

"I didn't keep it," I said. "Its mother wanted it back."

"She should be arrested for child abuse," Mac said.

"It wasn't really that tiny," I said. "It was probably three or four years old."

"When does your plane leave?" Mac said.

"I'm all right," I said.

"You know," he said, "I read in the paper that there's a seminar this weekend on getting in touch with angels. We could both go."

"You don't listen to me, do you?" I said.

There was silence in California, and then he said, "You threw out Timmy's blankie?"

I closed my eyes. "Mac," I said.

Mac sighed. "I'll tell you something," he said. "I hope I die before you do."

"I'll bury you in this town if you do," I said.

"A fate worse than death," he whispered.

I knew he was looking out his living room window at the sky above San Francisco Bay, just as I was looking out my mother's window at the sky above the garage.

"Most of them are," I said.

Convocation

On Thursdays Judith had her daughter, who had often threatened to commit suicide if Judith failed to love her sufficiently.

"You can't possibly understand my life," Rain said at about two o'clock every Thursday afternoon. "You just want to control me. You *want* me to die."

Judith would sigh and try not to look at her watch. The van came at four-thirty to carry Rain back to the halfway house, leaving Judith free to wash her hair and spend the evening decompressing in front of the television, so she could go back to her own life on Friday.

"I never thought life would turn out like this," she said to Dickie every Friday morning over coffee at the Village Inn. "I really didn't expect it. Did you? Did you ever have any idea?"

"None," Dickie said. "I thought my mother would be hale and hearty into her nineties, and then die in her sleep." Instead, Dickie's mother, old Mrs. Partee, was bedridden, suspicious, and vague, just alert enough to weep when Dickie showed up late for his daily visit.

"I'm about at my wit's end," Judith said. She poured herself more coffee from the never-empty pot and sat stirring sugar into it. "I'm damned if I do take care of her and damned if I don't."

"You're worse off than I am," Dickie said. "At least my mother's statistically likely to die before I do. I may have some time to myself before I gork out."

It was some satisfaction to know that Dickie thought her situation was worse than his, but it also made Judith feel guilty. "It's not that I don't love her," she said.

"I know," Dickie said, smiling.

Dickie Partee was a hairdresser who was four feet eight inches tall. He was said to have a remarkable way with wayward hair, but Judith had never gone to him. They had met after sitting through one meeting of a support group together; in the parking lot afterwards each heard the other heave a tremendous sigh of relief, and they burst into laughter and went out for a drink. Now they had a routine—two hours a week over coffee, and no holds barred when it came to mothers or daughters.

Judith had sometimes thought of moving away, but as time went on it seemed more and more unlikely. It was convenient that the van made the weekly run into town, making it unnecessary for her to drive up to the city to fetch Rain for her visit.

"You wouldn't even *see* me if it weren't for the van," Rain would accuse Judith on Thursday afternoons as they walked back to the clinic, to catch the van back. "You just better keep voting for higher taxes so the county will keep the service running." She sounded delighted at the idea that her mother would have to pay more and more.

"Oh, honey," Judith would say, kissing her good-bye and brushing—even though she tried to refrain—her daughter's bangs away from her eyes. "Now call me when you get home, and you have a good week."

"Oh, Mummy." Rain would shake off Judith's hands and jerk away, springing into the van and sitting on the far side. The driver would slide the door closed behind her and wink at Judith, which always started Judith back on the path to cheering up. The van settled as he climbed in, and the engine started, and as the van started to pull away, Rain would suddenly scramble into the backseat, her sullen, angry face crumpled into tears, and press her hands against the window in frantic good-bye waves to her mother. As the van carried her baby away, Judith would weep herself, waving her handkerchief, her heart growing lighter as the van grew smaller and smaller and finally turned the corner and was gone.

And besides the convenience of having her daughter delivered practically to her door once a week, she liked the town. She could walk anywhere, except to the mall, where she didn't want to go anyway. After coffee with Dickie she walked to work, crossing Washington Street and striding down Elm to College Place, where she turned and plunged under the maple canopy of the campus arboretum and slowed down to drift through fallen leaves, or bee-laden flowers, or squeaking snow, depending on the season, to her office.

There were only two problems with staying here. One was that her office was in a prize-winning newer building that had been cleverly designed by an architect who had never heard of either below-zero weather or soundproofing. Half the year Judith was forced to keep her moonboots on and wear fingerless wool gloves, as if she'd just come in from ice-fishing. And the acoustics of the building were such that she knew most of the professional secrets, and many of the personal ones, of Professor Arvin, even though he was on the other side of the building and downstairs. They were attached by some convolution of heating vents. That Professor Arvin knew her secrets, too, she could tell by the way he either caught or avoided her eye during faculty meetings, when various topics came up.

The other problem was that after a nationwide search the college had turned its bleary eyes toward home, and Dreiser Smith, her former husband and Rain's father, had just been named president of the college. It was unlikely to be a major problem; Judith herself stayed out of campus politics as much as possible, and Dreiser would considerately pay as little attention to her as he found consistent with their respective positions.

That was how he put it when he called her, soon after the search committee had approached him with the offer. "I just wanted to let you know, Judith," he said. "I don't foresee that it will be uncomfortable in any way."

"No," she said, "I don't imagine you do."

"Jude," Dreiser whined then, "don't be that way."

"Congratulations, Dreiser," she said, relenting a little. "What an honor." To get a job no one else in the country would take, she didn't add.

"I'll have a chance to do some of the things we've always

talked about," he said, sounding for a moment like the young instructor Judith had fallen in love with.

"Good luck," she said dryly. "I suppose Impy is quite proud."

Dreiser hesitated a moment, probably, she thought, trying to decide whether Judith was being sarcastic or not. In keeping with his new position he apparently decided to assume the best, and said, "Impy's pleased, of course; but she's so caught up in her own work that I'm afraid this will be quite an imposition on her time."

"I don't imagine she'll let it be, will she?" Judith said. "Her duty to God comes before her duties as first lady, doesn't it?"

"It's not as if she has a parish of her own yet," Dreiser said. "I would imagine she can make arrangements if she feels it's necessary."

"Well," Judith said, "I know Rain will be quite proud."

"Oh, yes," Dreiser said. "I'll have to let her know."

He was, really, as good a father to Rain as it was probably possible to be under the circumstances. As good a father as an administrator with no psychological insight, who thought that any person could *shape up* if he or she really wanted to, could ever possibly be. He spent an afternoon with Rain once a month, like clockwork; he paid his share of the bills that Medicaid didn't cover; and Judith suspected that because of Rain he had even declined to have a child with the young and fecund-looking Impy, thus causing her to turn to Christ for consolation. Judith did not *know* this last, but she thought it very likely, from the fierceness with which Impy sometimes shook her hand.

• • •

"So," Dickie said, the Friday after Dreiser's appointment had been announced, "the big man's reached the pinnacle. Aren't you sorry you gave all that up?"

"If I was still married to him, they never would have given him the job," Judith said.

"From what I hear, the priestly wife made them think twice," Dickie said, refilling his coffee.

"Nonsense," Judith said. "She's perfectly charming."

"My source says she's just a shade too earnest," Dickie said. "They think she'll try to convert all the alumni."

"Episcopalians don't convert people," Judith said. "Besides, it's her nature. It seems to me she was fairly earnest when she went about seducing my husband."

"Takes two to tango," Dickie said.

"You're right," Judith said. "I rather earnestly drove him into her arms." And she changed the subject.

Judith did not talk much about Dreiser or Impy to Dickie. All that was too long ago and had hurt her too deeply to discuss with anyone. Impy was just the proverbial blond girl student, albeit one who was now turning into an Episcopal priest. Judith mentioned them sometimes in passing, but only lightly, or with a roll of her eyes, and Dickie responded just as lightly; and they went back to Judith's daughter, or to Dickie's mother, or sometimes to their imaginary futures, when they would be free.

Rain had her ups and downs. As long as she took her medication, she was a joy to have around. She would go shopping with Judith, or to a chamber concert, and if they met any of Judith's colleagues she was as charming and forthright as any of the adult children who came back to town to visit their aging parents.

The problem was that Rain hated her medication. Judith could tell if Rain had gone off her meds as soon as she saw Rain's face through the window of the van on Thursday mornings, and her heart would drop like a stone into the bottom of her stomach.

"Don't you see, Mummy, that's not *me*," Rain would say when she was calm enough to discuss it. "I start to miss the voices."

"I don't understand that," Judith would say hopelessly. "How on earth can you miss them?"

"You're as bad as Daddy!" Rain would shout then. "You don't want to understand me! You don't even like the real me!"

But Judith thought she did understand what Rain meant; the bright, erratic, shimmering Rain was much more like Judith's old healthy child than the calm one that agreeably swallowed her pills every morning. But the drugs made it so much easier for Rain to function; no voices, no visions of hell, no people on the street conspiring against her and sticking out their demonic tongues. How could someone choose fear and, well, insanity over the easy chemical path through life?

"She is an adult," Dickie would say. "She's not stupid."

And Dickie was right; he was repeating Judith's own words. Rain was twenty-six years old, and she was brilliant. Just because she couldn't stick to anything, or concentrate, didn't mean she was incapable of making her own choices.

"Okay," Judith said. "*Mea culpa*. It's just so much harder for *me*."

"Right," Dickie said, and he laughed. "Same with Mom. *She's* perfectly happy as long as they don't turn off her TV. Why should I worry?"

"Would your mother really know if you didn't come to see her?"

Dickie rolled his eyes. "That's the question I torment myself with at night. It would probably make not one iota of difference to her. My visits are like trees falling one by one in the forest. No one even knows they go."

"Except the trees themselves," Judith said. "And eventually so many trees fall that there's no forest left."

"There's something incredibly heavy in that," Dickie said, "but I think it may take me a lifetime to figure out what it is."

Judith had long ago relinquished the embarrassing secret hope that a man unlike Dreiser would show up on her doorstep, begging to take care of her and her mad daughter. But sometimes she still dreamed of an uncomplicated companionship with someone who, when Rain left on Thursday afternoons, would walk home with her through the lengthening shadows, swinging her hand, and, when they got inside the door of their own house, heave a deep sigh of relief, pin her to the wall by her shoulders, and say, "Let's go out for Thai, beautiful." Or pizza, or Greek. But such a man's turning up was about as likely as Dickie Partee's growing twelve inches overnight, or Rain's showing up on a Tuesday to announce, "Guess what, Mom! I'm cured!"

Judith was not a person who had friends. There was Dickie, and of course she went to lectures and concerts with colleagues, and attended her share of cocktail parties and retirement dinners, but she did not have any what she would call *close friends.*

"I blame myself," Dreiser had once sighed when Judith pointed this out to him in what she had thought was an objective fashion.

"Yourself?" Judith had said. "Of all the things to blame yourself for, why choose my personality?"

"Because I'm so socially adept," he had explained. "You neither feel the need nor have you developed the skill to make friends."

This had silenced her, as so much about Dreiser had silenced her: his self-centeredness, his attitude toward their daughter even before her illness struck, his very strange way of seeing the world, as though, if only he had been consulted, the world would not be in such bad shape. It was not so much ego, Judith had finally decided, or even optimism, as it was a profound lack of understanding of what made people tick.

"Oh, come now," he had said to her when she ventured to tell him this, sometime toward the end of their marriage. "Your own field isn't exactly psychology."

"My field?" Judith said. "You think people's fields are all they understand?"

"You know what I mean, Judith," he had said.

"Anthropology is not entirely unrelated to human beings," Judith said.

"And where do you put God in all this?" he had said, looking at her over the reading glasses he had recently begun to wear.

"What on earth does God have to do with it?" she had said, astonished; and it was at that moment that she began to suspect that something was going on with Dreiser that she had never dreamed of.

Sure enough, a few weeks later, there, casually dropped on Dreiser's bureau beside his keys and a well-used hankie, was the letter from Impy. The letter did not mention God, but Impy did write that she felt blessed to know Dreiser, and the way she capitalized "Know" seemed significant to Judith.

The rest of that year was as tawdry and painful as years like that usually are. But it was the year after, when Dreiser had married Impy and was on sabbatical with her in Italy, that fifteen-year-old Rain's illness washed over them all, upsetting— none of them dared to say *ruining*—what they had all started to plan for the rest of their lives.

Rain had been named Sarah, but when she got sick she told her mother that everything was now changed. "Sarah is dead," she had said, weeping, as she lay on the table in the emergency room where Judith had brought her. "I am clouds, I am storm, I am cold gray Rain." And Rain was all she would answer to.

"What?" Dreiser had shouted from the distant continent. "Rain? You're calling me about the weather?"

He had refused to come home after that first episode, because it was, after all, a professionally important semester for him as well as a honeymoon with the blond Impy. "I can't rush back because Sarah's had a tantrum," he said. "She's jealous, *that* much I understand, Judith. She's a big girl now. She'll have to get used to the idea that Daddy's not always going to be available."

He had grown disgusted with Judith's calls, her descriptions of Rain's changed behavior. "*Make* her clean up her room," he'd said. "Tell her she's grounded until she straightens up. Don't let her go out on any dates."

"She doesn't have dates, Dreiser," Judith said. "She doesn't comb her hair and she doesn't bathe. Why would anyone ask her out?"

"Throw her in the shower, for God's sake," he said. "That's your department, not mine."

"Those years left me absolutely bruised," Judith told Dickie. "I thought I was crazy. Everyone dismissed what I said, as if I were a child or an imbecile."

"You know," Dickie said, "unless someone's lived with a crazy person, they just don't understand it."

"I'll tell you one thing, I know what Anita Hill went through," Judith said. "I would sit there describing Rain's behavior, and then some white-haired man would say, 'She'll snap out of it. Maybe we should talk about what's going on with Mother?'"

"Oh, my," Dickie said, burying his face in his little hands. "You poor thing." He looked at her through his fingers. "Speaking of Mother..." And they were off into his side of the story. She wouldn't eat, she demanded drink, she accused Dickie of stealing her money and keeping her a prisoner in the old folks' home. "Oh, God, Judith," Dickie said, "what would I do without you to talk to?"

"Talk to yourself," she said. It struck them both as hilarious, and they sat in the Village Inn shaking with laughter as their coffee grew cold and their waitress looked at her watch and stepped into the kitchen for a cigarette.

Well, they had all gotten used to it. Used, that is, to never knowing for sure where they stood, or what would happen tomorrow. And to the knowledge that they would never, any of them, be *quite* happy. Moments, maybe hours, maybe even days of happiness might occur, but in general they had to find their satisfaction in understanding that they were doing the very best they could, under the circumstances.

Human beings were so adaptable, Judith thought. The unthinkable so quickly became the accepted. The first few weeks in her new office, for example, she had been driven crazy listening to Professor Arvin's sneezes, and to his humming as he put his books on the new shelves and hung pictures on his walls. She had furiously called the Buildings and Grounds people, who referred her to the heating plant, who sent her to the chief of operations, who finally came up to her office and heard Professor Arvin's sneezes for himself, and said that perhaps the architect could redesign the air-moving system. And a week later Judith realized that not only did she not mind anymore when Professor Arvin sneezed, she had begun to hum along with him when she knew the tune.

And no doubt Rain was right—there was no way Judith could really understand her life. Rain was the one who had the voices and visions; she could never get away from them, never go to a movie or on a honeymoon or spend a night at the office in order to escape them, because they were always there. "The drugs make me dopey," she told Judith, "but the voices are *in* there. They're just dozing, waiting around. They know I'll give in in the end and let them come back."

The same thing had happened with Impy. Judith had hated the very thought of Impy for months. When Dreiser and Impy came back from Italy she had felt like running off to Antarctica, someplace where she would never have to see them. She had dreaded the first faculty party, the first concerts and plays and football games of the year, because she would have to see Dreiser and Impy together. But then she *did* see them, at an afternoon reception for a visiting historian. And although Impy was quite pretty, she was so very *young!* Of course, by now she wasn't young anymore, and over time Judith had come to rather like her, in an odd and uncomfortable way. Impy was part of her life, as much as Dreiser was.

That was the other thing—how easily people forget details. Living with Dreiser had often been difficult, but now she was hard-pressed to remember specifics, or, if she did remember them, to bring back the desperate and helpless feeling she'd had at the time. The Dreiser she knew now could have been an entirely different person; the removal of intimacy between them had changed not only the situation but the people in it.

Everything that fall seemed crystal clear, brighter and closer than it had for some time. The brilliant red and yellow leaves were untouched by crusty brown edges or spots; the children

Judith passed as she walked to campus were nicely dressed, their hair combed, their clothes sturdy, and they smiled politely at her and said, "Good morning"; the high-school band, marching past her house in the dark on the way to a football game, played in tune and with a heavy pounding of percussion that caught in Judith's chest and excited her, the way such things hadn't excited her for forty years. Perhaps, she thought, she was nearing menopause. But more likely it was the mild stress connected with the vague excitement on campus that made her feel more alert, a little on edge, a touch apprehensive.

The imminent anointment of the new president—even if it was just Dreiser—affected the whole college. Administrative assistants were busy planning a great, symbolic ceremony and accompanying gala events; the deans of things stood around in little knots in the halls, discussing the possibility of revamping lines of communication and authority; even individual faculty members, beneath the collective veil of academic cynicism, felt tiny surges of optimism at the thought that this or that long hoped-for but long despaired-of pet project—a new course in Hispanic lesbian literature, an increase in the number of physics hours required for graduation, perhaps a dental plan—might at last be put into effect.

There was just a slight awkwardness in Judith's position, an inhibiting factor when it came to candid discussions of the new president's proclivities and failings. When she walked into the faculty lounge she felt just a touch on *display*, as if people had just been saying, "I wonder how Judith feels about all this," but nobody quite had the nerve to ask her.

• • •

"Daddy called," Rain said over the phone. "He asked me to come to his inauguration and then he had the nerve to say, 'If you think you can behave.'"

"Oh, dear," Judith said.

"Why can't he think of *me* for once?" Rain said. "Why can't he even imagine how I feel?"

"He's that way with everyone, honey," Judith said.

"Behave myself!" Rain said. "What does he think I'm going to do, stand up and start shouting? Rip off my clothes and dance around in the aisles?"

Judith laughed. "He means well, sweetie. It's just that it's a very important day for him. He's worried about everything."

"He thinks I'm insane," Rain said. "He said Impy's giving the invocation. Do you think she'll wear her priest outfit?"

"She's not ordained yet," Judith said. "But the faculty will be gowned, so I suppose she will, too."

"I think I'll wear scarlet," Rain said. "Spangles and feathers. And dye my hair purple."

"If you want to, dear," Judith murmured. She had learned long ago that maternal protests sometimes made idle threats into stubborn promises.

And in fact when Rain arrived for the inaugural weekend, Judith was ashamed to realize how relieved she was that her daughter had brought a perfectly nice dress, red but unspangled, and that her hair was the familiar honey brown with golden highlights that she had gotten from Dreiser.

Saturday night Judith went to a dinner for Dreiser and

Impy, and when she got home a little after ten every light was on and Rain was taking a shower in the upstairs bathroom. Judith sighed and wished again that Rain would now and then do the dishes or turn out a light when she left a room. She turned off the television and locked the doors, and thought about the dinner. It had begun as a strained gathering of alumni and faculty on their best behavior, and Dreiser's rather stiff personality had dominated the room; but after Dreiser and Impy left, the party had livened up, and people had danced and drunk and conversation had been loud and loose, and Judith had found herself flirting with Professor Arvin.

As she stood in the dark living room and stared out the window, a car pulled up in front of the house and Impy got out. "Good Lord," Judith said aloud, and she went to the front door and opened it.

"Judith!" Impy said, stopping on the top step. "I thought you might be asleep."

"Well, I'm not." Judith led her into the living room and turned on a light. "Impy, what's the matter?"

"I wrote it all down," Impy said. "Dreiser doesn't know I'm here. If you were asleep, I was just going to leave it in your mailbox."

"Impy, what are you talking about?" Judith said.

Impy took a deep breath and sat down on the sofa. "Well," she said, "I'm about to be ordained a priest."

"Yes," Judith said, sitting down across from her. "Congratulations."

Impy shook her head. "My spiritual adviser—my confessor—

and I believe that I should enter the priesthood with my soul as unburdened as possible. And with all the important things going on this weekend—well, I thought this was a good time." She looked damply at Judith. "I need your forgiveness, Judith."

"Good Lord," Judith said. "For what?"

Impy looked down at her hands. "I knew Dreiser was married when he first asked me out," she said. "And I went anyway."

"Oh, for heaven's sake," Judith said. "That was ten years ago."

"Time doesn't change it from being wrong to being right," Impy said. "I'm afraid you were terribly hurt because of me, and I want to apologize."

"Impy, I really don't want to discuss this," Judith said.

"We don't have to discuss it," Impy said, wiping her cheek. "I just need you to forgive me."

Judith had never felt further from forgiveness than she did right now. She had never realized that Impy was such an incredible boob. "Oh for God's sake," she snapped, and suddenly she thought that the shower had been running since she got home—she looked at her watch—over an hour ago. She stood up, said, "Excuse me a minute," and ran up the stairs.

She knocked on the bathroom door. "Rain?" There was no answer. She tried the knob, but the door was locked. "Rain? Honey?" She knocked louder, and a slice of fear tore through her heart. "Rain!" she screamed, and she shook the doorknob with both hands.

"What's the matter?" Impy said, running up the stairs.

"Rain!" Judith cried, rattling the doorknob. "Help me open this."

"Oh, God," Impy said, and she threw herself clumsily against the door and bounced off. "Is there a window?"

"No," Judith sobbed. "Call someone. Hurry."

"Nine one one," Impy cried. "Where's the phone?" She rushed down the hall in the direction Judith pointed.

"Rain!" Judith called again through the door. If she could just get Rain's attention, she thought, she could keep her from slipping away. "Rain!"

"They're coming," Impy called, running back.

"Oh, God, let them hurry," Judith said, and she thought, I suppose Impy will think I'm praying. She pressed her ear to the door. It seemed to her that she could hear voices in the shower: conversation, and an occasional laugh.

Impy leaned against the door beside her, and together they pounded and called, "Rain? Rain?"

It was an eternity before they heard the siren, although it turned out later to have been no more than four minutes. Impy ran down to open the door, and Judith heard her saying, "Oh, hurry, hurry!"

Two policemen ran up the stairs. "Stand aside, ma'am," one said, and Judith jumped back as the men hurled themselves against the door. It broke with a crash, and sweet moist air burst into the hall as they ripped away the splintered plywood and plunged into the bathroom.

Rain, standing in the shower trying to cover herself with her arms, screamed.

One of the policemen, with what Judith later thought was

remarkable presence of mind, took a towel off the rack and held it toward Rain, turning his head away.

The other one reached in and turned off the water. "Are you all right, miss?"

"Of course I'm all right," Rain shouted, clutching the towel.

"Why didn't you answer me?" Judith said angrily, wincing at the harsh sound of her own voice.

"I didn't *hear* you," Rain said, wrapping the towel around herself. Judith saw that she was covered with goosebumps, and her lips were blue. The hot water had run out long ago.

Two emergency medical technicians had run up the stairs and stood behind Judith, looking into the bathroom. The policemen stepped out through the broken door, both of them holding their hands up as if they were subduing a mob.

"Just a misunderstanding," one of them said to the ambulance attendants, but Judith felt he was giving her a dirty look as he said it.

"You're kidding," one of them said.

"I'm sorry," Judith said. "I made a mistake." She stood looking at Rain as Impy went downstairs with the four men.

Rain had cut off most of her hair, and what was left stood up in wet purple spikes. "What did you think I was doing, Mummy, slitting my wrists?" she said, stepping out of the shower and adjusting the towel.

Judith burst into tears. "You didn't answer," she said. "I called you and called you and you never answered. I never know what I'll find."

"Oh, Mother," Rain said irritably, and then she too began to cry. "Neither do I. I wish I was dead."

"No you don't," Judith said, putting her arms around her.

"Daddy will never forgive me."

"Of course he will," Impy said, appearing at the door.

"You don't understand," Rain cried angrily. "My father has never loved me."

A great wave of fatigue washed over Judith. "Rain," she said, "stop worrying about Daddy."

"But it's true," she said.

Judith looked at Impy over Rain's head. "It's not true," she said at last. "And if it were, purple hair isn't the way to win his heart."

Rain snickered in spite of herself. "Oh, Mother, what am I going to do?"

"You'll just have to let it grow."

"But I can't *go* tomorrow," Rain said, weeping again. "I can't let anyone see me this way."

"It won't wash out?" Impy said.

Rain shook her head. "I've been washing it for hours."

"You could wear a scarf," Judith said.

"Oh, right, Mom," Rain said, rolling her eyes. "Show up in a babushka. That wouldn't attract attention."

Judith looked at her watch. "Maybe I could call someone."

"Who?" Rain said.

"A hairdresser I know," she answered.

"It's an acceptable fashion in New York," Dickie said,

walking around Rain and examining her head.

"I hate New York," Rain said.

"Do you think you can do anything?" Judith said from the doorway. "Make it less extreme or something?"

"Sure," Dickie said, "we can do something."

"Glue my hair back on," Rain said.

"Honey, Dickie can't work miracles," Judith said.

"He has to," Rain said, twisting around in her chair to look at him.

"You don't need a miracle," he said. "You just need a good haircut."

"And a dye job," Rain said. "I want my normal color back."

"That I can't promise," he said.

Rain turned around again and closed her eyes. "Don't touch my hair if you can't fix it."

"Rain," Judith said. "Dickie has come all the way over here in the middle of the night to help you. Do you have to be so rude?"

"Mother, this is my *life*," Rain said. "I feel so fragile right now, I'm just not responsible." She buried her face in her hands.

Judith shook her head at Dickie and beckoned him out into the hall. "I am so sorry," she said in a low voice. "I apologize for her rudeness."

Dickie shrugged. "I'm a hairdresser," he said. "I'm used to it."

"I just don't know where the line is," Judith said. "Is she really fragile, or is she just spoiled? Even after all these years I don't know what to do."

"You're talking about me!" Rain called. "Stop talking about me!"

Dickie patted Judith's arm. "Why don't you leave us now, Mother," he said, and he grinned. "Go have yourself a nice drink with your friend."

Judith went reluctantly downstairs. She couldn't imagine what Dickie could possibly do to salvage Rain's hair, and she was sorry she had called him. He would never forgive her for dragging him into this. And Rain would twist it all around so that Dickie's failure would be the root of all the trouble and it would be her, Judith's, fault. Proving once again that she didn't really love Rain at all.

In the kitchen Impy was hanging up the phone. "I called Dreiser," she said. "I told him everything was under control."

"Why on earth did you call Dreiser?" Judith said.

Impy looked surprised. "It's nearly one in the morning."

"I hope you didn't tell him about Rain."

"Well," Impy said, "I had to give him some reason for being here."

Judith started to say something, but she thought better of it. She got a bottle of wine out of the refrigerator, and they sat drinking silently at the kitchen table until Rain called, "Here I come!" from the top of the stairs. With a look at each other, Judith and Impy went out into the hall.

Rain was marching down the stairs, her hair a mere dark shadow spreading over her skull. In spite of herself, Judith put her hand to her mouth. It was like seeing a vision of her daughter in death, the skin around her ears gleaming, her bones sharp under the thin white bathrobe.

Rain stopped halfway down. "Well?"

With her hair gone, there was nothing to distract from her marvelous green eyes. What a funny thing, Judith thought, to forget how beautiful your own child's eyes are. "Rain, darling, you look lovely," she said.

"She's got the cheekbones for it," Dickie said as he came down behind Rain.

"What do you think, Impy?" Rain said.

Without hesitating, Impy said, "You look beautiful," and Judith forgave her everything.

Rain and Dickie came on down the stairs. "What are you doing here, anyway?" Rain said to Impy.

But before she could answer there was a knock at the front door and Dreiser walked in. "What's going on here?" he said, and then he saw Rain and said, "Good God."

"Hi, Daddy," Rain said. "It's the cancer ward look."

"Cancer?" he said, and Judith saw a look of terror cross his face.

She started toward him, but Impy said, "Darling, it's a *fashion*," and moved over to kiss his cheek.

"It's all the rage in New York," Dickie said.

Dreiser looked down at Dickie, and Judith watched with awe and amusement as his social skills clicked into action. "I don't believe we've met," he said, extending his hand. "I'm Dreiser Smith."

"Dick Partee," Dickie said. "Congratulations on your big day tomorrow."

"Thank you," Dreiser said. "Are you an alumnus?"

"No," Dickie said, "I'm a hairdresser."

"I think I know your mother," Impy said.

"You do?" Dickie said, looking up at her in surprise.

"Mrs. Partee? Out at the Vercingetorix Nursing Home?" Impy said. "She always speaks very highly of you."

"She does?" Dickie said.

"Oh, yes," Impy said. "In her clearer spells she doesn't talk about anything else."

"Is that right," Dickie said, and a look that Judith had never seen came over his face. It was a slow smile that rose from his mouth into his cheeks, brightening his skin as it went, and it lit up his eyes and the tips of his ears, and even the scalp that showed between the dark strands of his thin hair, as if a floodlight inside him had been turned on.

Judith felt odd the next day. It may have been lack of sleep, but as she filed into the chapel and sat down in the front pews with the rest of the faculty, everyone seemed insubstantial and miles away. She might have been watching big-screen TV as Impy, her golden hair almost too bright to look at against the black of her gown, spoke a brief and, to Judith, incomprehensible prayer. Her eyelids drooped as trustees and alumni spoke, and then she perked up again as Dreiser was sworn into office, his hand resting on a Bible that Impy held. It seemed to Judith like Kabuki theater: a performance that had a great deal of meaning in some context, but not in hers.

She watched as Dreiser swept to the podium in his black gown and scarlet hood to begin his speech. He looked excited; he was probably very happy. Over in the choir alcove Impy sat in rapt attention, and beside her was Rain in her red dress, with the red velour belt from Judith's bathrobe tied around her head. She looked terrible. Probably everyone who saw her thought she *did* have cancer. Judith could imagine the comments—"All the trouble with that girl and now *this*." Maybe that's why people seemed so interested in Dreiser's speech— the bald daughter and the priestly wife made him a more sympathetic character.

She wondered if another hairdresser might have been able to do something less drastic with Rain's hair. Just bleach what was left of it blond, perhaps. Maybe Dickie had been mad about being called out in the middle of the night, and had taken it out on Rain to get back at Judith. Dickie had probably thought it was just a bad haircut, not a matter of life and death at all.

When she ran up the stairs to her daughter last night, Judith had been convinced that the strange thing she'd felt all fall was a change in Rain, in her behavior or in her body chemistry; something that Rain herself was unaware of, a subtle clue that only Judith could detect, as mothers recognize the smell of their own babies as soon as they're born. But as she leaned on the door beside Impy, Judith had suddenly known that it was a change in *her*, herself. She was tired. And even if she could call Rain back this time, it might be the last time; she no longer had the strength to keep the world from collapsing.

So when the police broke open the bathroom door to expose Rain standing naked in the ice-cold shower, washing her hair, it was the happiest moment of Judith's entire life. It was the moment she would have chosen to live in forever: a flooding

119

instant when everything she had ever wanted was granted, and she loved her daughter absolutely, just as she was—naked, screaming, and purple-haired.

Judith glanced around at the faculty. Everyone appeared to be absorbed in what Dreiser was going on about. But perhaps they weren't listening to him any more than she was; they were lost in their own thoughts, planning lectures or vacations, or getting up the nerve to ask someone out, a blond girl in one of their classes perhaps. As she looked around she saw that Professor Arvin was watching her from down the row. Before she could look away, he crossed his eyes at her.

She tried to stifle her laugh, and it came out as a horribly loud snort. Heads all around turned to look in her direction, and Dreiser faltered in his speech for a moment. She bowed her own head and fumbled in the sleeve of her gown, hoping she would find an old Kleenex from a long-past graduation; she didn't, but the new physics professor sitting next to her took a clean white handkerchief from her purse and handed it to her.

Judith held it over her face with both hands and sat hunched over as Dreiser droned on and on. She tried not to shake or to make any noise. Maybe people would think she was overcome with emotion; maybe they couldn't tell if she was laughing or weeping. God knew, most of the time she couldn't tell herself.

Almost Home

for Hans

There's a lot of tragedy in the universe that has missing parts and comes to no conclusion, including probably the tragedy that awaits you and me.

— Norman Maclean, *Young Men and Fire*

Before Bob killed the rooster it had been in the yard for a week, popping out of the woods at odd times to stand near the pump house and crow, waving its stumpy wings. The thick feathers on its neck dwarfed its tiny head; it seemed to have no eyes at all. Once when it appeared in the yard Bad Cat sprang after it, but the rooster flew squawking and shrieking onto the roof of the shed, where it walked around nervously clucking to itself. After that, each time it showed up Decker shooed the animals inside, and they sat at the window with their ears up, watching the rooster stroll around the yard with its feathers undulating.

Until the last day, when the rooster made a brief appearance at the gate and Bob saw it before Decker did. Bob charged, and the rooster flew into a tree where it clung precariously to a thin branch before losing its balance and flying to the ground to run screaming through the trees with Bob hot on its heels. Decker shouted hopelessly into the woods, and after a few minutes Bob appeared trotting along the stream, his tail waving high and a dead rooster in his mouth.

"Drop it!" Decker shouted, and Bob *did* drop both rooster and tail, and slunk toward Decker to be beaten and sent inside for the rest of his life. He kept his ears down all afternoon, but his eyes remained smug little predatory slits, and he kept licking his lips.

Decker got the shovel from the shed and trudged out through the woods to where the dead rooster lay head down in the creek. Bob hadn't ripped any of the rooster's skin; he had probably broken its neck. Decker still couldn't really see the head on the creature: just a beak, a red comb, and, among the sodden bright orange feathers, a closed eye.

When Decker picked it up by the legs, his knuckle grazed the sole of its foot, and he was surprised at how soft it was. He walked along the stream, the rooster dangling upside down, until he stopped at a wide flat place on the bank, where he laid the rooster down and dug a hole. The soil was easy to dig, and after he chopped through the root of a madrone, he had a hole big enough for the rooster to rest comfortably in. He would have liked to save a couple of its feathers as a remembrance, but when he tugged gingerly at a tail feather, it gave no indication of coming out without a struggle, so he just laid the rooster in its grave and shoveled the dirt over it. He pulled a log over the spot so that Bob wouldn't be able to dig it up.

Decker was shaken by the death of the rooster. The rooster had been so—well, so *ridiculous*, strutting out of the wild woods into the yard, bobbing around with its tiny head, crowing foolishly to announce its presence. It had looked absurd up on the shed roof; it had looked completely out of place perched in the tree where it had first flown to escape Bob. The bravado of a stupid domestic bird like that, attempting to live in the woods on its own; and then attempting to join Decker's household. So brave, so stupid! It was enough to make a strong man weep.

"Hell, the damn woods is full of roosters," Bear Franklin said when Decker told him about it at the Family Mart, standing in Frozen Foods. "One less rooster makes no difference."

"Well, maybe," Decker said. "But it's the idea of my dog, too. Bing! Just like that he goes wild."

Bear shook his head and leaned close to Decker, shaking a box of frozen puff pastry in his face. "Dogs and women," he said. "They smile and lick you all over and roll on their backs, and the next thing you know they've offed something in the woods." He stood back and dropped the box in his cart. "Can't trust a one of them."

"Bear," Decker said, "what do you do with that puff pastry?"

"Chicken pie," Bear said. "Makes all the difference in the world."

As he drove home Decker thought about what he'd said to Bear. Maybe that was what really bothered him so much: Bob's abrupt transformation from pet to predator. Maybe that was what *he* feared sometimes, living here: on the edge of the woods, at the far side of town, up a dirt road away from other houses. His cat was half-wild, his dog was beginning to revert, and at any minute he, too, could slip over the edge and do something violent.

He shivered a little as he thought of how easy it had been to pick up the rooster by the feet. In the past he had wept at things like that. Dead creatures, crippled things, pigeons mourning beside their flattened friends in the road. The very thought of an injured animal had been enough to set him off. But when Bob had come trotting merrily out of the woods with the rooster flopping in his mouth, Decker felt nothing but anger. There it was: Bob had done a violent act and it had stirred Decker not to pity or grief but to anger.

Decker had moved to the woods to get away from violence, but he'd known right away, the first week, it hadn't worked. Every day he could hear gunshots echoing down the canyon. He felt better when they came in volleys, because then he was sure it was somebody shooting at bottles or NO TRESPASSING signs; but when there was a single shot followed by silence, Decker tended to close his eyes and shudder, because he thought that someone had probably just shot a deer, or a raccoon, or even a skunk. For all that, someone could have just shot a woman walking her dog, or a person picking mushrooms in the wrong place.

Bear and Velveeta Franklin were the first people who had befriended Decker when he moved up here. In the front yard of the Franklins' house were dozens of rocks with "HELP! TURN ME OVER!" painted on them. The first time Decker went there for supper he bent over and picked one up. On the other side it said, "THANKS! THAT FEELS BETTER!"

"Aren't those darling?" Velveeta said from the porch. "I saw those in a craft shop over in Sweet Home one time and I couldn't stop laughing."

Decker followed her into the kitchen. Velveeta taught crafts workshops, and the house was filled with grapevine wreaths and toilet tissue carnations.

Bear was sitting at the table peeling potatoes. "*Pommes frites*," he said, holding out a wet hand and shaking Decker's dry one.

"*Parlez vous francais?*" Decker said, accepting the beer Velveeta handed him.

"*Un peu*," Bear said. "I used to sell chickens to the Hmong over on the coast and the closest we ever came to communicating was in French. Little did my high-school French teacher know I'd be talking to gooks in her precious language."

"Honey," Velveeta said, sitting down at the table with them, "I'm sure Mr. Decker doesn't call them gooks."

"You in Nam?" Bear said, looking up at Decker from under his bushy eyebrows.

"No," Decker said. Bear was gazing expectantly at him, so Decker said, "Asthma." He left out the part about running up and down the stairs of his doctor's building while smoking a cigarette.

Bear nodded and resumed peeling, and Velveeta said sympathetically, "That why you moved up here?"

Decker shook his head. "Just for the quiet, really. Get away from the city."

"You said it," Bear said. "Me and Velveeta came up here for the same damn reason. Out of the rat race." He carried the bowl of potatoes over to the counter, where he placed a pale potato in the middle of a cutting board. He pulled a huge square cleaver out of a drawer and, holding it in front of his chest, bowed to the potato. Then he raised the cleaver above his head and screamed, "Hai!" bringing the cleaver down with a *whump* into the cutting board. The potato fell into two perfect halves and lay quivering on the board.

Velveeta reached over and patted Decker's hand. "Zen," she whispered. "After Nam he really got into it."

"Chop chop!" Bear shouted, and another potato bought the farm.

Decker was reheating a cup of coffee when he looked out the window to see Bob lying on his back, happily waving his legs, and Velveeta bending over scratching his stomach. Decker stepped back from the window as she straightened up, but she saw him and waved. He went out on the porch.

"Bear told me about your rooster," she said as she came up the steps. Beyond her Bob was lying with his feet in the air, gazing after her with his tongue hanging out of his mouth. "That's a sad thing to have happen."

"It wasn't my rooster," Decker said. "It just came into the yard."

Velveeta shook her head, smiling. "There's something you should know about me," she said. "I'm a little bit psychic."

"You are?" Decker said. He suddenly remembered the cup

of coffee in the microwave. "Would you like some coffee?"

"I'd love some," Velveeta said, following him inside. "I can sense things that other people can't."

"I hope you don't mind reheated," Decker said.

"Not at all," she said. "I could sense that about you the first time you came over."

"That I would serve you reheated coffee?" Decker said.

"That you're more sensitive than most men," Velveeta said. "Than most *people*. Women aren't any more sensitive than men, in the general scheme of things."

"Cream? Sugar?"

"Black," Velveeta said.

"Let's sit outside," Decker said. He led the way across the yard to the wooden swing.

"I don't think things just happen, either. There's usually some reason behind it."

"Like wish fulfillment, you mean? Freudian slips?"

"That's one of mankind's first attempts to explain fate through science," Velveeta said. "It's a clumsy attempt, but it's a step in the right direction. Let's get down to specifics." She shifted on the swing so that she was facing Decker, and she leaned toward him, tapping his bare knee with her fingernail. "One. Why do you think you moved here?"

"Peace and quiet," Decker said.

She shook her head. "That's the superficial reason," she said. "The truth is that there is a lot of energy concentrated here right now. A *lot*. People are being drawn here from everywhere for a purpose."

Velveeta's skin was grainy and there were wrinkles at the corners of her mouth. Her black hair was riddled with white, and a large swath of white hair swept away from her left temple, seeming to draw that side of her face away from the other side, so that Decker had to keep looking from eye to eye to feel sure that he saw her whole face.

"Two," she said. "Why did that rooster come to you?"

"Bear said the woods are full of roosters," Decker said.

"He did?" she said. "Where are they, then?" She sat back and looked at the woods behind the house, and Decker did, too, expecting to see dozens of roosters scuttling about through the trees. "I think someone is trying to get a message to you."

Decker laughed. "Why don't they just call me on the phone?"

"One of the problems with this society," Velveeta said, "is that skepticism is trained into all the wrong people, for the wrong reasons." She put the palm of her hand on Decker's knee. "God works in mysterious ways."

"God sent the rooster?" Decker wished he could think of a polite way to remove her hand, which had begun to gently knead his knee. He was afraid she would squeeze too hard, and he would scream and jerk his leg away, thus spilling tepid coffee over both of them.

"What do you know about your former lives?" Velveeta said, sitting back and crossing her arms.

"Velveeta," Decker said, "I don't want to hurt your feelings, but I don't believe in that stuff."

She smiled. "That doesn't hurt my feelings, Decker. Because it really doesn't matter what we believe. The truth goes marching on whether we fall in step or not."

"Well," Decker said, "you've got a point there."

Velveeta stood up. "Thanks for the coffee." She leaned toward him, putting her hands on his shoulders, and he stood awkwardly with a cup in each hand as she gazed into his eyes. "I'm glad you're here, Decker," she said.

Velveeta's visit left him feeling strangely expectant. He stared out the window, and every time Bob's toenails scritched along the floor, or a jay screamed in the woods, he jumped. He kept peering into the woods, looking for the shapes of foolish roosters. But nothing happened, except that Bad Cat threw up a live lizard under the bed and then ate it again before Decker could get it away from him.

Gradually Decker relaxed, and the vise of anxiety in his chest eased. The expectant feeling she'd roused in him settled into the bottom of his lungs and lay there for a while, sluggishly rising up when something scurried through the fallen madrone leaves out back, but when nothing was there the feeling turned around, grumbling a little, and lay down again.

That night he gave in and called Miriam.

"Well, you *are* blessed," she said when he told her about Velveeta's visit.

"They seemed like such nice people," he said.

"Just because they have some sort of religious belief doesn't mean they're not nice," Miriam said. "Religion's a comfort, Decker."

"Not to me," he said. "The thought of being a chess piece is not a comfort to me."

"You've made a religion out of not having any," she said. "You certainly seem to take comfort in thinking we sprang from the Serengeti."

"It makes more sense than believing I'm here because of some mysterious energy," he said. "I don't feel any energy."

"Neither do I," she said. "But then I work eight hours a day."

"I guess you're mad at me," he said.

Miriam was quiet for a long minute. "I'm not mad at you, Decker," she finally said. "I just don't see any point in continuing."

"I'm sorry I called," he said.

"Me too," she said.

Decker went outside. There were more stars in the sky above his ten acres than he'd ever been able to see in the city, but they weren't crystal clear; there was always a haze in the air— smoke from burning slash, or the humidity put off by respiring trees. It had been stupid to call Miriam; it just made him feel worse. He half suspected that she had begun to move toward some kind of religious belief herself. It would be just like her, to go over to the believers, and leave him out here in the cold.

The next day Marlowe Cramm came to fall and buck the dead fir that threatened Decker's roof. Decker's land was second or maybe third growth. He'd found a couple of very large and fat oaks in the back, and a couple of very big madrones, one of which his neighbor to the north subsequently cut down and carried off for firewood, even though it was very clearly on Decker's side of the property line. But the firs and the pines were none of them very big; they were tall, a hundred and more feet, but they were thin as pencils compared to what they could be. Decker would have preferred to live in a sacred sequoia grove somewhere, where man had never yet set foot, but that was just his own idea of heaven, and he knew it was pie in the sky.

"Ordinarily, a snag that size, maybe fifty bucks," Marlowe Cramm said as he craned his neck to peer at the top of the tree. "But seeing's you're a friend of Bear's, make it thirty." He looked sideways and down at Decker, who was bent over holding on to Bob's collar.

"Thirty bucks?" Decker said. "Are you kidding?"

"I got kids to feed," Marlowe said stubbornly.

"No, no, that's fine," Decker said. In the city it would cost a couple of hundred bucks to have a tree that size taken down, but as soon as he spoke, he saw a sly grin ease into Marlowe's cheeks.

Marlowe slipped on his ear protectors. "Better stand away," he said loudly. "No guarantees when it comes to trees."

Decker moved back a few steps, pulling Bob along with him, and Marlowe pulled at his chainsaw a couple of times before it roared into life. He stepped up to the dead fir and slid the tip of his instrument into it once, twice, and made a little V-shaped cut. Then he moved around to the other side and held the full edge of the blade against the bark. Without hesitation the chain buried itself in the wood, and ten seconds later the huge old snag began a slow-motion descent. It hit the ground like a bomb. Marlowe stepped up to the fallen tree and neatly cut it up into stove-length sections. Five minutes and the job was done.

"Looks so easy," Decker said.

Marlowe pulled off his earmuffs. "Huh?"

"That's some job," Decker said. He let go of Bob, who bounded over to the tree and began to examine it in great detail.

Marlowe pulled a pack of cigarettes from his shirt, offered one to Decker, and lit one for himself. "It's man's work, I'll tell you that," he said. "You know what? You ever watch a woman try to fall a tree?"

"I don't believe I have," Decker said.

"You won't, either," Marlowe said. He stood smoking, looking at the fallen fir.

"A check okay?" Decker said.

"I'd prefer cash," Marlowe said. "If you got it on hand."

"Sure," Decker said. He pulled his wallet out and handed Marlowe three tens.

"I don't trust banks," Marlowe said. " 'Course, what difference does it make? They got the money marked."

"Marked?" Decker said.

"Sure," Marlowe said. "Microchips. They can trace every bill."

"Who?" Decker said.

"Don't be naive," Marlowe said with a smile. He slipped the money into his shirt pocket behind the cigarettes and headed for his truck. He climbed in and looked down at Bob, who was peeing on the front tire. "You ever hunt that dog?"

"No," Decker said.

Marlowe ground out his cigarette on the outside of the door and stuck the dead butt into his pocket along with Decker's three bills. "He could be trained." He raised his hand and started the engine. "Take it easy."

"Hear that, Bob?" Decker said. "You could be trained."

Bob said nothing.

He spent the afternoon rolling the pieces of falled snag one by one up to the side yard, where he stood them on end and split them into firewood. "The muscles in his brawny arms rippled as he brought the mighty sledgehammer down," he said aloud. "It seemed effortless, a smooth flow of energy from somewhere deep in his loins up through his body and out into the long blunt instrument. Each blow drove the steel wedge deeper into the wood, as if it were soft as a mealy yellow potato."

He raised the sledge high over his head again. "Hai!" he screamed, and slammed it down. The section of fir stood still for a long second before it fell apart like a sigh and lay back in two pieces on the ground.

"It looks just like the Catskills in these pictures," Myron said.

"It's hotter here," Decker said. "It reaches a hundred degrees fairly often."

"A hundred degrees," Myron said. "I can see the appeal, though, living in the wilderness."

"This isn't exactly wilderness," Decker said.

"Decker," Myron said, "let an old man have his fantasy. It's closer to wilderness than I ever was."

"Well," Decker said, "to tell you the truth, me too." It was true. He had never been into a designated wilderness. He was well aware that he took a certain comfort in knowing that he was close to a road or a utility line; he was ashamed at knowing that he would be a little frightened, a little nervous, out in the wilderness.

"I give you one full year," Myron said.

"You're a city boy," Decker said. "You have to remember I grew up in a very small town. I don't need constant entertainment."

"One thin year," Myron said.

"Is there some reason you called, Myron?" Decker said.

"Miriam worries about you," Myron said. "She'll never say a word, but she loves you."

"Myron," Decker said, "I really don't want to talk about this."

"I'm not young anymore," Myron said. "Decker, I'm eighty years old. What's going to happen to me?"

"Come on, Myron, you're in good health."

Myron blew a deep sigh down the telephone line. "Sometimes I wish I wasn't," he said. "Sometimes I wish I was dead."

"Yeah," Decker said. "I know how you feel."

"Come back," Myron said. "We can go to the movies together."

"Myron, what's going on?" Decker said. "Have you seen Miriam lately?"

"She loves you, I know she does," Myron said.

"Okay," Decker said. "Don't get upset. You know I can't come back, Myron."

"I understand that," Myron said. After a minute he said,

"Sometimes I wish you had called me Dad. You'd say, 'Dad? I'll call you back,' and I'd have to chuckle as I hung up."

"Myron, I'll call you back," Decker said. "Even better, you can call me anytime. Meanwhile, call Miriam. She'll want to talk to you."

He hung up and went to the window. A deer was walking slowly past the fenced-in vegetable garden, eyeing the tomatoes. Bob lay on the porch, his chest rising and falling. Decker could almost hear his snores. He wished he could do something for Myron, but he couldn't. He couldn't do anything for anyone.

His life would just sort of continue to trudge along. There was nothing wrong with that; he wasn't one of the quietly desperate, he was free enough of entanglement that his head was above the crowd, and he could see fairly clearly in most directions. But in the end that made no difference. It was all very well to scoff at religion and the meaning of life, but without them a man didn't have much leeway; when you didn't feel up to living as part of a vast evolutionary scheme, there was precious little left to keep you going.

Decker let Bob out one evening and he didn't come back.

"Bob," Decker called into the night for hours. "Bob!" He might have walked into a bear trap, or fallen down a ravine of some sort and broken his leg, or been killed by a mountain lion or one swipe of a bear's heavy paw.

"Bob!" he called again in the morning, but heard no barking, no jingling of license tags, no panting and scrambling through the leaves. He walked through the woods all day, coming back to the house periodically to see if Bob had come home, but only Bad Cat sat on the porch, staring at him indifferently.

Decker had always thought it was irresponsible of people to lose animals. He couldn't bear to think of Bob lost, wandering through the woods getting hungrier and hungrier, full of sorrow and bewilderment that Decker would treat him this way.

"Decker!" he imagined Bob calling in dog language. "Decker!"

Decker put photocopied signs on telephone poles all up and down the road, but they yellowed and tore and dimpled in the dew, and there was no trace of Bob. Night after night he left food out on the porch in Bob's dish, and every morning it was licked clean, but he knew it wasn't Bob, it was skunks or raccoons or the stupid cat who had eaten it. Decker had never been a cat person, and now Bad Cat was all he had left.

"Lost your mutt, huh?" Bear said when Decker went down to the farmers' market one Saturday. He was sitting in a lawn chair between a madrone-flower honey booth and a woman selling chocolate cheesecake. Behind him was his pickup, piled high with crates of garlic.

"I'd appreciate it if you kept your eyes peeled," Decker said. "If anybody hears anything."

Bear looked up at him with his pale unblinking eyes and smiled. "Sure," he said. "I'll keep my nose to the ground."

"A lot of garlic," Decker said, looking at the truck.

"Turkish elephant garlic," Bear said. "Best food known to man. Cures the common cold, cancer, herpes, and AIDS."

"AIDS?" Decker said.

"The government has suppressed the evidence," Bear said. "The best way to cook it is dig a pit, put in a dozen heads, and cover them with rocks. Build a fire on top of them, throw on more rocks, and then slap mud over them. When the mud's rock-hard and dry, dig them out and eat them. Smooth as a baby's ass and just as sweet."

"Sounds exotic," Decker said.

"They taught me that in Turkey," Bear said. "All this"—he waved his hand at the truckload of garlic—"is from one clove of garlic I brought home from Turkey in 1973."

"Incredible," Decker said.

"I was on the road for years after Nam," Bear said. "I didn't feel welcome in my own country."

"Those were hard times," Decker said. He hadn't felt particularly welcome himself.

"Something inside me was busted," Bear said. "I went all over Turkey, Algeria, India, looking for answers."

"Did you find any?"

Bear's eyes narrowed a little. "I found out how goddamn primitive other cultures are. I was glad to get back to the USA."

Decker nodded. "We live lucky lives."

"Bool sheet, muchacho," Bear said. "Nothing lucky about it. Hard work is what it is. Chug!" He reached behind Decker to shake the hand of an old man who had rolled up in a wheelchair. "How's it hanging?"

"Nothing between me and the grave but life itself," Chug said.

"You know Chug Cramm?" Bear said to Decker.

Decker shook his hand. "You related to Marlowe?"

"Marlowe's daddy, in the flesh," Chug said. "Named him after a detective but he never has figured that out."

"Decker here lost his dog," Bear said.

Chug shook his head sadly. "Woods is full of lost dogs," he said. "Body parts, too. I lost my thumb and both my legs to the timber industry. And then my wife run off to join Earth First!" He looked up at Decker. "Whereabouts you lose this dog? Hunting?"

"He's not a hunting dog," Decker said. "He just disappeared in the night from my yard."

Chug tipped his head back and looked knowingly down his nose. "Dogs and women," he said, and his nostrils flared. "They sniff something new and off they run, with never a thought for the hand that feeds them. Tell you what, though." He pointed the forefinger on the thumbless hand at Decker's heart. "A dog shows up again, you take him back. Good dog's worth something."

Decker smiled.

"Come hunting with us," Chug said. "Lost dogs hear the shots and come running. It gets in their blood."

"You still hunt?" Decker said, eyeing Chug's empty trouser legs.

"Hell yes," Chug said. He looked back over his shoulder, then leaned toward Decker. "Most of the time I just shoot from the cab. Illegal as hell."

"Most of the time," Bear said, turning back to them, "we just go out there and party."

"Three, four days in the woods and we go home with pickled peckers," Chug said. "Don't matter much for me, but these married men have hell to pay. You a married man?"

"No," Decker said. "I'm not."

"Gay?" Chug said.

"No," Decker said.

"When I was in the service my whole squadron was fairies," Chug said. "They was straight shooters and they stuck by their buddies. Plus, they wasn't no competition when we liberated those little French villages." He shook his head solemnly. "There's two sides to every tale, that's what I say." He reached up and thumped Decker on the shoulder. "You come hunting with us. You don't have to shoot anything. We'll show you a good time and look for your dog."

"Thanks," Decker said. "Thanks for asking me."

"I like you," Chug said. "You look to me like a man with a good heart."

Decker drove slowly home, the bag on the seat beside him filled with elephant garlic. It was good to have friends, he thought, but they weren't everything. Once you had friends in a place, you were caught in a web of obligation—not so much to entertain them as to stop and talk to them when you met them in the road, or to buy cookies made out of sawdust from their children, or to delight in their vegetables during the summer when you thought you'd scream if you saw one more tomato coming up the walk.

What I am, he thought, is a man with a good heart and a stupid cat. If only Bob had been able to leave a note. He could probably come across the smell of Bob's last message right there at the base of a ponderosa pine.

> DECKER. AM LIGHTING OUT.
> SEE YOU NEXT TIME AROUND.
> LOVE, BOB.

Maybe that's what the rooster had been trying to tell him, Decker thought. "Bob will dis-ap-PEAR."

The phone rang as he walked in the door. "It's Daddy," Miriam said. "I think it's his heart."

"What do you mean you think?" Decker said.

"*He* thinks it's his heart," she said. "He won't go to the doctor and he won't get out of bed. He says he wants to die."

"So let him die," Decker said. "He's lived a full life."

"Decker, how can you say that?" she said.

"Miriam, he's done this before," Decker said. "What does he want?"

"You," she said. "He lies there with his eyes closed, and tries to lift his hand, and says in a faint voice, 'Decker? Decker?'"

They both burst out laughing.

"One of these days," Decker said, "Myron will have cried wolf too often."

"That's easy for you to say," Miriam said, "but what am I supposed to do?"

"He's your father," Decker said. "I can't tell you what to do."

She sighed. "Maybe if you called him."

"Maybe." He waited a second and said, "Bob's gone."

"What do you mean, gone?"

"He just disappeared from the backyard," Decker said. "One guy thinks he might have been stolen for hunting."

"Bob?" She laughed. "Poor Bob, pressed into white slavery in the hunting trade."

"Spotted slavery," Decker said.

"Maybe he'll come back," she said in her comforting tone. "Maybe he took a vacation."

"Maybe," Decker said.

"Call Daddy, okay?" Miriam said.

"I'll call him," Decker said. "But I can't promise I'll be nice to him."

"He deserves what he gets," she said.

"You think so?"

"No," she said softly. "We none of us deserve that."

She's right, Decker thought, nobody *deserves* anything. Not home, nor happiness, nor a reason for living. And who could ever, really, deserve the bad things?

The phone rang again. "I'm so sorry about your dog," Velveeta said. "I know how close you were to him."

"Thanks," Decker said. "I guess these things happen."

"Well," she said, "I know that's your attitude, but there could be another explanation."

"You think he was stolen?" Decker said.

"Life is like a tapestry," she said. Her voice was a little muffled, as if she had the receiver stuck between her chin and her shoulder while she did something else with her hands.

Painted a rock, he thought, or fluffed some toilet paper into the semblance of a rose. "We have to give up looking for patterns with our eyes and try to see with the collective wisdom of the universe."

"My goodness," Decker said. "You think the wisdom of the universe would concern itself with my dog?"

"I can sense how upset you are," she said. "But I want you to think about something. Everything happens for a reason. We have to learn as much as we can before we're allowed to go on to the next step. You're experiencing a series of losses, small to start with but growing in importance to you. Like, the rooster you hardly knew, but your dog, he's more important. Maybe that's something you should think about."

"Maybe so," Decker said. "Thanks for calling, Velveeta."

"Good night, Decker," she said, and for a second, despite his irritation, he felt a flash of comfort, as if the universe was wishing him a good night in the voice of Velveeta.

He called Myron's number and a thin voice said, "Hello?"

"Myron," he said, "get out of bed."

"It's the middle of the night," Myron said. "Hello, Decker."

"What's going on, Myron?" Decker said. "Don't do this to Miriam."

"You ought to come home," Myron said. "It could be I'm really sick, really dying."

"Myron," Decker said, "your dying won't bring Sam back."

"If it would," Myron said, "I would die a thousand times. You know that, Decker."

"Yes," Decker said, "I know."

"He was the sunshine of all my days," Myron said. "The light of my life. The apple of my eye."

Decker said nothing.

"I know what he was to you, Decker," Myron said.

Decker sighed. "Myron," he said, "if there was any chance I could ever see him again, I would believe anything they told me to."

"Ah, Decker," Myron said, "you and I, we don't even have the comfort of an afterlife."

"No," Decker said. "Do me a favor, Myron. Get up. Don't give Miriam any more grief."

"There's something I have to tell you," Myron said.

Decker clutched the receiver. That particular phrase always gave him a chill. "What?"

"She's begun to date."

"That's great," Decker said.

"Worse than that," Myron said. "I think she's serious."

"She's always been serious," Decker said. "That's her personality."

"You're pretending to joke," Myron said. "Decker, I think she might marry this man."

Decker noticed that there was a great cobweb covering the jade plant in his kitchen window. How had it escaped his notice? "Is there something wrong with him, Myron?"

"Not that I know of," Myron said. "He seems a fine man. No religion. But he has two grown daughters."

"Well," Decker said, "that doesn't seem too terrible."

"Oh, Decker." Myron breathed heavily into the phone.

"What if she wants to have a child with this man?"

"That would be good for her, don't you think?" Decker said, hoping he sounded sincere.

"I don't want to go through it," Myron said.

"It would make you happy," Decker said helplessly. "It would make her happy." But knowing what she knew, an older and wiser woman, how could she possibly contemplate bringing a child into the world?

"It would bring her grief," Myron said.

"Myron," Decker said, "it's her decision."

"I know that," Myron said. "I just wanted to tell you."

"I know *that*," Decker said. "Sleep tight, Myron."

He went outside and sat down on the steps and stared into the darkness. An owl hooted clearly in the woods, over and over. It was there every night, hooting, trying to put the fear of God, or of Owl, into tiny mammals. The trees themselves were silent; not a breath of air stirred in the treetops.

The road curved around Decker's piece of land, making a peninsula of it, and he could hear a truck roaring along it. When it was close enough he could feel deep, heavy bass notes thumping out of its speakers. He imagined the windows open, the long-haired truck driver singing along, banging on the outside of the door with one hand as he sped through the forest. Decker hoped the small mammals would stay out of the road. Being snatched by owl talons was a much more dignified way to go than being flattened by truck tires.

The truck screamed past, and when it had died away Decker heard the distant songs of coyotes, yapping and howling at something in the night. Pleasure drifted into his chest as he sat listening to them. Maybe Bob had joined forces with them and was even now up on Mount Baldy, learning to dance in the light of the moon with an attractive little coyote bitch.

A sudden gunshot rang out, not so very far away, higher up, in the direction the truck had gone. The coyotes were abruptly silent.

"Ah, nature," Decker said, and he went inside to bed.

It was a summer without dog days. There had not been a great deal more rain than usual, but the clouds that convened over the valley hung there for days at a time, so that what little moisture there was in the air stayed around, sinking to the surface of the earth at night and rising into the trees by day. The leaves of Decker's strawberries had grown huge in their efforts to absorb sunlight. Numerous flowers were fooled into thinking it was still spring, and they bloomed dreamily on and on, imagining that summer was around the corner. Snow stayed on the peaks Decker could see in the distance; his eggplants had dozens of blossoms, but by August not one had set any fruit.

"El Niño," Velveeta told him, and he nodded politely.

But by August, despite the clouds and the recirculating dew, the forest was as dry as a tinderbox. The woods were full of great crashing sounds that turned out to be dead madrone leaves crashing into the piles of their brethren on the forest floor. When a deer walked through the woods, its dainty hooves could be heard for miles, crushing the fallen leaves and dried-out branches. Out in the meadows the chicory rose high and brilliant blue above the dead yellow and brown grass, and seed pods burst and scattered their seeds like shrapnel when Decker accidentally brushed against them in passing.

The pile of logs he had split was five feet high and fifteen feet long, stacked for the winter under the tin-roofed shed at the back of the house. By October, when he would start needing fires in the morning, it would be nicely cured and ready to go. Except for the bit of help he'd had from Marlowe Cramm, he had chopped it and hauled it and split it and stacked it all on his own, from his own property. He was very nearly self-sufficient, at least where fuel was concerned.

Decker would hear a couple of theories on how that summer's big fire started. One was that a spark jumped out of an illegal burn barrel outside somebody's single-wide and hit a ravine full of dead johnsongrass and that was that, the conflagration was on. The other theory was that somebody had pulled a trailer off at the side of the road and sparks from the muffler had lit the dead weeds. Or somebody might have fired a gun, poaching or target-shooting or just firing aimlessly for the fun of the noise, and the speed of the bullet whizzing through dry grass touched it off.

Whatever started the fire, it was afternoon when Decker heard helicopters chopping over his house, and he stepped outside to smell smoke and see a stream of pickups full of volunteer firefighters rush by on the road past his property and disappear up the hill. He looked up the hill and saw a great gray cloud of smoke above the trees. It billowed and bloomed, and when he got his binoculars and stared through them, he saw bits of flaming leaf flying in front of it. Then he looked around and saw that a layer of smoke covered the sky, and behind it the sun was fading to a dull orange.

A police car turned into his driveway and pulled up into the yard beside him. "Sheriff Floyd Peach," the driver said.

"Big fire," Decker said.

Floyd Peach nodded. "We've got instructions to evacuate the homes along this ridge," he said. "Right now the danger's not extreme but that wind picks up, we're in trouble."

"Evacuate? Really?" Decker said.

"Yes," Floyd Peach said, leaving no room for discussion. "Leave your garden hose hooked up in case the firefighters need to use it to protect your domicile. Then get on down into town. You got relatives to stay with, that's the best plan for now."

"Is there anything I can do to help?" Decker said.

Floyd Peach squinted at him suspiciously. "We advise untrained civilians to just clear out," he said. "There's a relief effort down at the state park off the interstate, though. They'll need help."

Decker watched Floyd Peach back his truck down the drive. Then he fetched down the cat carrier from the top shelf in the garage. "Bad," he said, "we have to evacuate the area." Bad Cat, who was sleeping on the dining table, opened one eye as Decker approached, and then tried to leap out of his reach, but too late. Decker seized him and stuffed him into the carrier.

He looked around. His books? His clothes? What precious belongings would he die without? He threw some underwear in a suitcase and put the suitcase and the cat carrier, with Bad Cat complaining inside, into the back of the pickup. He went out-side and connected the hose and coiled it up, and leaned his shovel against the house beside it.

Then he stood beside the pump house and stared into the woods. "Bob!" he shouted. A madrone leaf crash-landed at his feet. Something skittered through the undergrowth. A helicopter throbbed overhead, the heavy beat of its propeller thickening the rhythm of Decker's heart. The smell of smoke had gotten heavy. He thought he could hear shouting in the distance, crack-ling, the thrumming of engines, the shrieking of gears and the ripping of trees being torn up by bulldozers.

"Bob!" he called one last time. Surely the animals of the forest would be heading toward water. The roosters and the dogs would be following Bambi and Thumper and the little forest creatures, bounding and flapping and hopping and slithering toward the nearest creek. Animals were smart. Animals could take care of themselves.

"Bool sheet, muchacho," he said aloud, and he got into the truck and drove away from his house as Bad Cat yowled in the back.

The park off the interstate was crawling with volunteers. Women hauled great coffee urns out of their trucks, and old men set them up beside Coleman stoves. Children squealed and bounded among piles of bedding while the red-bellied tankers droned overhead, carrying tons of ammonium phosphate to bomb the flames with.

"Fire ain't nothing new around here," Chug said as he and Decker slapped paper-thin slices of ham onto white bread.

"What's new is how many damnfool people have built houses up in there. Half the time they ain't even in the fire district, and then they're pissed when the fire service don't come to put out their fires."

"What happens to them?" Decker said.

"They burn up," Chug said. He dropped an empty mayonnaise jar into a trash barrel and opened another one. "It ain't common knowledge yet but they already lost three houses. Every building at that wildlife rehab place, too."

"Wow," Decker said. "What happened to the animals?"

"The volunteers had to run through at the last minute and open the cages," Chug said. "Shooed 'em out into the woods. That grizzly, too."

"Lila la Griz?" Decker said. Lila la Griz had made national news last spring when she was captured in Montana after breaking into numerous summer cabins. She'd been trucked cross-country to Wildlife Haven, the only animal shelter willing to take her, and she'd spent the summer there in a pen, putting on weight.

"Hell," Chug said, "she won't last long. There ain't been grizzlies in this state for seventy years. She'll end up a rug in somebody's single-wide."

"Poor thing," Decker said.

"Well, who knows?" Chug said, kindly tapping his arm with the mayonnaise knife. "Where there's life there's hope."

For days truckloads of firefighters went back and forth, fresh and determined-looking boys heading out and sweaty, grimy men in blackface stumbling out of the trucks on their return. Decker stood beside Chug and poured endless cups of coffee and handed out dozens of sandwiches. The Family Mart supplied case after case of navel oranges, and a bright citrus smell sprang up among the odors of smoke and coffee and sweat as the firefighters peeled oranges and described the thundering booms of imploding trees, the scorching heat of the flames, the deadening labor of digging ditches and scraping firebreaks, and the heart-sinking feeling of watching the flames leap a fifty-foot break and head for somebody's manufactured home.

Then, full of food and exhausted, the firefighters would disappear into the tents that the base crews had set up, and for a while the voices thinned and the only sounds were the clanking of coffee urns being refilled for the next crew and the snoring of exhausted men.

Decker made his share of sandwiches. He hauled a load of garbage to the landfill and he took a turn doing laundry in the temporary laundromat that had been set up in a tent, and watched the gray water run out of the back of the half dozen machines down through a ditch into the river. He helped locate the lost mothers of sobbing children, asked about four hundred people to turn down their tape decks, and gave away kitty litter to six people who hadn't thought what a cat locked up in a trailer for a week might want to bring with him.

He slept in the back of his own truck, his face next to Bad Cat's cage. Bad, curled into an unhappy circle, opened his eyes briefly to glare at him and then closed them again. Decker lay unable to sleep for hours, the adrenaline that had been rushing around in his body still percolating. He pictured the blind and crippled birds and deer and cougars from Wildlife Haven rushing off into the woods, terrified by the shouting and the smell of the smoke. He listened to Bad Cat's small snores, and the other snores and restless movements from the tents and campers around him, and beyond them other noises—an owl, a barking dog, the endless throbbing of helicopters.

It was thirteen days before they got the fire under control. Finally the fire crews started being pulled out, and stompers went in to clear up and dig out and to oversee the dying down of the burning, which would not stop completely until the winter rains came. People got ready to go back to what was left of their homes.

On the last night Decker, standing at the edge of the park, closed his eyes for a minute. The screeches of the children had turned to exhausted wails, and now and then he thought he could catch the plaintive cry of Bad Cat from his own pickup, parked back under the trees. This, too, was nature, all this noise and running about. We are the only animal that can fight fire, he thought. We fight before we run.

Under cover of darkness he slipped past the state police who were keeping the rubberneckers on the move and walked down the highway until he reached the bridge where the river went under the road. He stepped over the guardrail and slid down the embankment. There was a narrow ledge that ran under the bridge along the bank of the river, and Decker inched his way in. In here the noise of passing cars was swallowed by the sound of rolling river water, sluggish though it was this time of year. It was pitch black under there and the stink of smoke was mixed with the odors of moss and fungi and the excrement of the swallows that nested up on the walls, and it all rushed up into Decker's nostrils. He kept his breathing shallow and with one hand on the wet wall he carefully moved into the darkness until he could see nothing. This was what blindness would be like—smells and sounds, cool wings and webs brushing against his face, his fingers sensitized to the smallest bump and knot, to the sharpness of edges just before he touched them, to the sudden softness of mud or muck or bat crap.

He stood still for a minute and slowly the blackness in front of him became paler, and the opening on the other side of the bridge took shape. He shuffled toward it and when the warm evening air hit his face he was taken by surprise. It was sharp with the stink of cinders, but he took in a deep breath of it and stepped out into the open.

He gasped. The fire had burned away from the river, up into the valley, and behind it the dark mountainside was covered with thousands of glowing shards of orange light, where drops of fire were burning themselves out. They pulsed slowly, or flickered in burning pools, and here and there they ran uphill in thin lines that he realized were brushy gulches that had been passed over by the earlier flames and were trying in vain to catch up.

Above the hills the smoke had cleared, and the whole black sky was filled with brilliant silver stars. Directly in front of him, resting smack on top of the burning mountain, was the Big Dipper. Four, seven, a dozen stars ran right down the sky as he watched, as if the Big Dipper were pouring them out onto the surface of the earth.

Without taking his eyes off the sky, he stumbled up the bank and across the parking lot to stand at the top of the boat ramp. He looked down at the water and saw with great delight that the spots of fire glowed there, too, shimmering oblongs and jagged lines that dimpled and stretched with the unhurried flow of the water. As he stared he became aware of a huge pale shape floating in the shallows. He stepped down the ramp until his toes were at the very edge of the lapping water and leaned over to peer at it.

It was a body, bobbing gently, face up in the river, and as Decker stared at it in horror, it suddenly opened its eyes and looked directly at him. Its mouth opened and a garbled scream bubbled out of it, and it flailed wildly, showering him with drops of cold river water.

"Aaag!" Decker heard himself scream, and he leaped away, foolishly flinging his arms up over his head.

The body rose up out of the river and stood silhouetted against the glowing hillside, water streaming off it in silver sheets. "You scared the shit out of me," it said.

"Oh my God," Decker said. "Bear?"

"Got it in one," Bear said. He shook his head, sprinkling the smooth water around him with a pockling of drops, and walked up the boat ramp, water sliding out of his hair and down his legs to run back down to the river behind him.

"I thought you were a dead body," Decker said.

"Technique I picked up in country," Bear said, holding up a plastic drinking straw. "Used to be I could lay underwater for hours, but I've lost my touch. I'd be dead meat if this was Nam."

They walked over to the bench overlooking the river and sat down. "All the time I was fighting the fire, all I could think of was laying underwater."

"Bad, huh?" Decker said.

"Never seen a fire that wasn't," Bear said. He stretched his arms up over his head and yawned. "What really gets me is the sound of the choppers."

"Flashbacks?" Decker said.

Bear shook his head. "Memories. Intense. See, in a combat situation you're *on* every second. I felt more alive in Nam than I ever have since."

"That's pretty sad," Decker said.

"I know what you're saying," Bear said. "But *I'm* saying, it didn't have to be Nam. It's the intensity of the situation, is what it is. You got a forest fire, you got yourself a damn intense situation."

"I guess so," Decker said.

Bear tucked his hands behind his head and stretched out his legs. "My boy would love this," he said.

"Your boy?" Decker said.

"Jimmy," Bear said. "He's got Down's Syndrome. Lives in a group home down near my first wife."

"Oh, wow, I'm sorry," Decker said.

"No, he's doing real good," Bear said. "He's a bagger at Safeway. He got Employee of the Month one time." He reached behind the bench for his clothes. "Agent Orange. I sued the hell out of the government, but it was dismissed. No proof, they said."

"Fuckers," Decker said.

Bear shrugged. "I cheat on my taxes."

Decker took a deep breath and said, "My boy died."

"Jesus," Bear said. "What happened?"

Decker noticed a small spot of fire on the hillside suddenly flare up and run uphill to join another, smaller pool of glowing flame. Together they burned brightly for a moment and then died down.

"I took him to McDonald's," he said. "He had just gone up to get more ketchup. I had some right on my tray but he wanted his own. So he went up to the counter by himself and he was just reaching up for the ketchup when this guy burst in the door with a machine gun and yelled something, and Sam—"

Decker looked up at the Big Dipper hanging steady in the sky. "I looked at Sam and he was just staring at the guy, his mouth hanging open, and then he looked back at me with the wildest grin, this light in his face. He was such a smart little guy. He wasn't scared at all. He thought it was TV. He thought something exciting was happening to him."

"Oh, man," Bear said.

"And then the guy let loose. And I'm yelling 'Let it be me!' Ha. Like the fucking song. 'Let it be me!' As if anyone could hear me."

"God," Bear said.

"He killed three children, an old man, and one of the kids behind the counter. And then the bastard killed himself. It was over in one minute. It was like nothing had happened. Just an accident of timing. If we'd gone to Burger King, it would never have happened."

Bear stood to pull up his jeans, fastened them and then sat again. The hair on his chest was still damp, and it glistened like gold in the light from the fires. "I love my son," he said, "but it ain't the life I thought it would be."

"No," Decker said.

"Tonight," Bear said, "before you came, I was laying there underwater watching the stars fall. And this just came into my head: Out of the wrack and ruin of our dreams of the frontier, a terrible beauty is born."

Decker smiled in the dark. "That's poetry, Bear."

"I know," Bear said.

The fire burned twenty thousand acres. Even though Decker's house was untouched by the flames, the smell of smoke had seeped into the towels hanging in the bathroom and the clothes in his bureau drawers, and it billowed out from between his sheets when he got into bed at night. He left the doors and windows open, and he and Bad Cat sat on the front porch for a week, staring at the birds poking disconsolately through the ashes across the road.

It was enough to drive any man to find a job.

"One thing," Sylvia Crane, Decker's boss at the Wildlife Department, said at the end of his one-day training session. "You do know about Lila la Griz?"

"Sure," he said.

"Does that worry you?" she said, gazing at him.

"Should it?" he said. He had read enough to know that a

grizzly would not be interested in him unless he did something very, very offensive.

"You don't want to do anything stupid," she said, "but no, it shouldn't worry you."

"Has anyone seen her?" Decker said.

"Not to my knowledge," Sylvia Crane said. "She's probably headed back to Montana." They looked at the half dozen maps tacked to the wall of Sylvia's office. "Grizzlies can travel a hundred miles a day if they want to, following their homing instincts."

"It doesn't seem very likely," Decker said, staring at the white spaces that were deserts and ski resorts, and the lines that were the interstate highways that lay between here and the grizzly's hope of freedom.

"Her chances are good," Sylvia said firmly. "Her chances are excellent."

And who was Decker to disagree with a professional? He hoped Lila would get home, too. If it would help to pretend to optimism, then he would pretend. Let all bears get home free.

So as Decker surveyed Fry Creek he was alert, but not what you would call frightened. He figured he made a hell of a lot of noise crashing through undergrowth and sloshing through water, when there was enough, and swearing when he slipped or got his shirt snagged on a branch. It was hard to believe anything would want to kill him smack in the middle of the day.

Decker liked this job. It got him out in the woods tromping around listening to birds and eating bear food, and away from people, except people like Harton K. Small, who owned thirteen acres along the creek and had answered his door carrying his rifle and said he didn't want any goddamned government employee setting foot on his land. Decker figured Harton K. Small was more likely to kill him than a poor old scared and lonely grizzly that had been liberated by fire, but he wore his cerise WILDLIFE DEPARTMENT hat and his blaze orange vest so it was clear he was official, and he parked his truck on the edge of busy roads so that if his mail started piling up Sheriff Floyd Peach would know where to start looking.

Anyway, minimum wage hardly made him a government employee. He was just out here to survey the stream.

There had been no precipitation at all yet, and everything was discouraged. Up here in the woods where the fire hadn't reached the oaks had simply stopped, the green fallen out of their leaves, which now hung brown and desiccated. Big-leaf maples gleamed a dull yellow here and there among the firs, and the ponderosa pines were dropping their brown needles on the forest floor. The only brilliant color was the red of the poison oak.

He climbed over a high clot of alder branches to find himself looking at a pond. He looked closely at the branches and saw that the ends had been neatly gnawed into points. It pleased him that beavers had managed to get this far up the stream, through the dairy farm and past the property of Harton K. Small, and dammed up the stream so that Harton K. Small's water was cut to a mere trickle. Harton K. Small was the sort of person who would come blow this dam up if he knew it was here. Decker was the sort of person who would not tell him.

He made his way over to the bank, walked through a tangle of willow and around the dam, and waded back in. He moved out into the pond, thrusting his walking stick around until he found what he thought was the deepest point, and the water came to the four-foot mark. He wrote that down, and then he wrote down the abbreviations that indicated the type of banks at the side of the pond, and what proportions of gravel and sand and cobble composed the bottom, and what the flora at the edge of the water was: alder, willow, and overhanging blackberry.

He inched over and ate several handfuls of the overhanging blackberries, which were fat and sweet and perfectly clean, lacking in road dust or pesticide. "Just the meal for a hungry grizzly," Decker said aloud. He laughed but he stepped away from the edge, and waded on till the pond shallowed out into puddles and then became a stream again.

He came around a bend in the stream and there in a clearing was an old green trailer with a couple of lawn chairs and a card table set up beside it. Hunters, probably. Bear season opened tomorrow.

"Hello!" Decker shouted, just to be on the safe side. There was no guarantee that a hunter loaded with alcohol would realize that bears didn't speak English, but it didn't hurt to talk. "Hello there!"

Sure enough, the trailer door swung open.

"Sorry to bother you," Decker shouted. The stream was small, but its water made just enough noise that it swallowed his voice. "Just doing a stream survey. Wildlife Department!" He waved his clipboard.

A woman stepped down from the trailer and walked over to the edge of the stream. She was wearing a blue stocking cap from which wisps of white hair stuck out, and she carried a rifle. "You hunting?" she shouted.

"No!" Decker shouted back, shaking his head vigorously. He took off his hat and pointed to the WILDLIFE logo. "Doing stream surveys! Salmon habitat!"

The woman nodded and turned away. Halfway back to the trailer she looked back and shouted, "Just leave the fucking bears alone!"

"Okay!" Decker waved his hat and grinned like an idiot. "Okay!"

Flourishing his pencil, he waded on up the stream without looking back at the trailer. His was not to wonder why. Most of these woods were BLM land, which meant that they were more or less public and that people used them as they saw fit. All along Fry Creek, for example, there were mining claims, a few of which had been worked and had left piles of rock and sand to wash down into the water, but most of which were simply used for vacation camps, like the one that trailer was parked in.

Scattered here and there through the woods there were piles of trash, too, Pampers and coffee cans and burnt-out refrigerators. Last week he had come upon the rusted carcass of an old car riddled with bullet holes, smack in the middle of the stream. Its shape had reminded him of the old white Ford his father had driven in the fifties.

And in one spot, where the creek ran along a private meadow, he had stumbled across a little grassy island where half a dozen blue pails sat not quite hidden in grass and honeysuckle, and in them grew the first marijuana plants Decker had seen since he graduated from college. They were extremely healthy. The young couple who had given him permission to walk through their part of the stream had obviously forgotten their little crop. He hoped they wouldn't let someone *really* official walk through, but he had never gotten back to warn them.

A slim shadow swept along the sandy bottom right in front of him. He stopped and peered into the water, where a long shape had tucked itself into the curve of a boulder. He wrote it down in the comments column—CHINOOK, 12 INCHES. As he went on up the stream he pictured the fish's whole life: hatching from an egg in the gravel of the stream, and living as a tiny fry in the gravel and cobble streambeds until it was big enough to head out to sea; then coming back, not only past natural waterfalls and beaver dams and the wading feet of herons, but through the obstacles men put in its way—fleets of fishing boats, nets stretched across the mouths of rivers, concrete dams with useless fish ladders, silt-filled streams, flatwater bearing jetboats and rafts and hundreds of sports fishermen. And as far up Fry Creek as it could get, it would lay its own eggs and die.

He remembered then that among the terrors of protecting children from all harm lay the extreme pleasure of showing them fish and leaves and sunlight, the things he himself liked.

The *putt-putt-putt* of rotors bounced back and forth across the canyon and a government helicopter came out from behind the trees overhead. It followed the creek and then hovered right above him, and Decker could see a face peering down through the Plexiglas. He waved, and a hand waved back. They were looking for Lila la Griz.

He went slowly upstream for another half hour, stopping every few feet to measure a width or a depth and write it all down on his waterproof data sheets. The shadows had gotten very long by the time he finally reached the road he'd been aiming for, a little dirt track that forded the creek and would lead him back to the gravel road where he'd left his truck. He sat down and pulled off his boots, and then struggled out of his waders. The air was cold but the neoprene waders were hot, and his shirt was soaked with perspiration. Another couple of days and he should be able to finish this stream. Bear season ran for a couple of weeks, and then deer season opened. Decker wasn't too keen on streaming when the forest was full of men with loaded guns.

As he headed back to the main road, a pickup came around a curve and pulled to a stop beside him. Bear Franklin rolled down the window. "Saw your truck," he said. "Thought you might be around here."

"Just heading home," Decker said. "What are you doing out here?"

Bear grinned. "They had a griz sighting up here last week. We are going after big fucking game."

"Aren't grizzlies a protected species?" Decker said.

In the passenger seat Marlowe Cramm snorted and leaned across Bear to look at Decker. "You run into a griz in the woods, you ain't going to stop to think about no Endangered Species Act."

"I suppose not," Decker said.

"Hell," Bear said, "she's long gone anyway if they saw her here last week. Them bears make tracks."

"Maybe, maybe not," Marlowe said. "If she found our bait barrel, she's got reason to stick around."

"Whyn't you come on back to camp with us?" Bear said. "Chug's making chili. We told him we'd bring you if we found you. Stay overnight."

"I don't have any gear," Decker said.

"We got extra," Bear said.

"I'm not a hunter," Decker said.

"Daddy makes a mean chili," Marlowe said. "Don't hafta hunt to appreciate that."

"We'll take you back to your truck in the morning," Bear said. "We got a shitload of beer."

"Well," Decker said.

"Great," Bear said. "Hop in. We're just going down to restock the bait."

Decker threw his daypack in the back of the truck and squeezed in beside Marlowe, who handed him a beer.

"Too bad you lost that dog," Marlowe said. "It would've made a good bear hound."

"Bob wasn't a hunting dog," Decker said. But today he liked the idea of old Bob out in the woods hunting; gutting and skinning a rabbit and throwing it into a cauldron over a campfire, and as the rabbit stew bubbled merrily and dark descended, throwing his head back to howl at the rising crescent moon. It was better to think of Bob that way than as starved, or injured and helpless, or cowering in the hollow trunk of a fir as the fire raged around him and smoked him to death.

"Acclimates 'em," Marlowe explained to Decker when they had parked and were walking down through the woods toward the bait barrel. He had hauled it into a canyon along the creek during the summer, and he had made the trip up to keep it stocked with bait every couple of weeks since then. "They get used to being served. Then hunting season rolls around and *blam!* Ol' Mr. Bear is dead meat."

"Speaking of dead meat," Bear said, pulling a green bandanna out of his jacket and holding it over his nose.

"We're getting close," Marlowe said.

The stink got so strong Decker could almost see it hanging in the road. They rounded a curve and saw the barrel, a rusty fifty-gallon drum, lying on its side, and around it were scattered some long bones and a thing that might have been a strung-out intestine.

"We've had customers," Marlowe said with satisfaction. He righted the barrel and emptied one of the bags he carried into it. Out fell a whole cow's head, the eyeballs clouded white but intact, the tongue lolling out between its teeth.

Then he opened the other bag and poured out a dozen Hostess Ding-Dongs. "They love these," he said. "You don't hardly need the meat, but it don't hurt to cover all the bases."

Bear gagged.

"You okay?" Decker said.

Bear, still holding the handkerchief bunched up over his nose and mouth, nodded. "I've just never got over the smell of death," he said in a muffled voice. He and Decker walked slowly back toward the truck, and when they'd gotten away from the stench, they stopped to wait for Marlowe.

"Normally, I'm a fastidious man," Bear said. "I hate to see people's shit all over the forest." He removed his hankie and sniffed experimentally; satisfied, he tucked his handkerchief back in his pocket. "But when I go hunting it's like civilization doesn't exist anymore. It's like you're out in the woods, in nature, and *pow!* your primitive instincts take over." He finished his beer and tossed the can into a ravine.

"So you litter?" Decker said, watching the can roll down the hill.

"It's like stripping down before a fight," Bear said. "Like meditating. Getting rid of all the extraneous baggage, till it's nothing but you and your prey." He looked gravely at Decker. "It's a religious experience."

"Bear burgers, here we come," Marlowe said, running up behind them. "Oh, man, we are going to live high this winter."

"In Asia they pay thousands of dollars for one liver," Bear said. "You ever had bear liver pâté? You try it once, you're hooked."

"I don't believe I've ever had chili this spicy," Decker said, blowing his nose again.

"Have another beer," Chug said. His wheelchair was wedged in between the little sink and the fold-down table. "My mother was pretty hot-blooded, to tell you the truth. She had mixed Mexican and Cherokee blood. And *her* mother—your great-grandmother, Marlowe—now, she made a chili that burned your tongue."

Bear popped the tab of another beer. "In Guatemala they grow a chile that's so hot they can't even harvest it without heavy gloves. They soak it for two days and then use just the water to cook with, and even that's so hot they don't let niños and gringos eat it." He closed his eyes and then opened them again. "My tastebuds burned off when I first ate it and they didn't grow back for a month."

"How come they let you eat it? You look like a gringo to me," Marlowe said.

"I spent some time down there," Bear said. "After a while they accepted me."

"Now, I can't see doing that," Chug said, taking another plate of chili from Marlowe. "Going to live in some foreign culture."

"For a long time after Nam that was my way of life," Bear said. "It was the only way I could stand to live."

"Yeah, that's when they got started on this new world order," Marlowe said. "All those peace talks in Paris? The pope was right in there with Kissinger and the Rothschilds."

"The Rothschilds were in on the Paris peace talks?" Decker said.

"Marlowe's got that bee in his bonnet," Chug said. "He always did have a big imagination."

Marlowe swallowed his mouthful of chili. "You a religious man?" he asked Decker.

Decker shook his head. "No," he said. "Not at all."

"That's good," Marlowe said. "Because organized religion is a crock. You have to go straight back to the Bible, man. It's all there in black and white."

Bear looked up from his plate and raised his hand. "Did you hear something?"

"Like what?" Decker said.

"A clunk," Bear said.

"I don't hear nothing," Chug said.

They sat, straining to hear.

"There," Marlowe whispered.

They heard a sort of hissing sound, and then a scuffling noise outside the door.

"What the fuck," Bear said, standing up, but before he could move, the camper door popped open and the woman Decker had seen earlier along the stream stepped up onto the threshold. She was dressed in olive drab fatigues, and her face was blackened with camouflage makeup. She was holding her rifle and she looked slowly around the trailer, staring coldly at each of them.

With her free hand she unhooked a radio from her belt and said into it, "I'm in. They're unarmed."

A woman's voice crackled back, "Ten-four."

"Of course we're unarmed," Chug said, slamming his beer down on the table. "We're eating our damn dinner."

"That godawful chili your mother used to make, by the looks of it," the woman said.

"Angela, you've lost your mind," Chug said in disgust.

The woman put her radio back on her belt and looked straight at Decker. "You," she said, "were warned."

Marlowe stood up. "Mom, put your gun down."

"Sit down, Marlowe," she said.

Marlowe sat down.

"What damnfool thing are you up to, Angela?" Chug said.

"I've told you before," she said. "You mess with the bears, you answer to me."

"Threatening people with guns ain't exactly legal," Chug said.

Angela snorted. "Men's laws are sins against the universe. Anyhow, we don't take lives, we stop the immoral taking of lives." She shifted her stance, hugging her rifle a little closer. "We will stay here until bear season is over, and then we will be here to stop the immoral killing of deer, and then the immoral killing of elk. You might as well give up. Your hunting days are over."

"This is just a bid for attention," Chug said to Decker.

"There's enough of us to stop every hunter in this state," Angela said. "And I might as well warn you, we have no fear. We will protect the lives of our fellow beings with our own lives. You shoot at them, you'll hit one of us."

"Mom, come on," Marlowe said.

"Quit whining, Marlowe," she said. She looked around at them again. "One more thing. Lila's under armed escort. Harm one hair on her body and there's likely to be a serious hunting accident in these parts." She lifted the gun and shot out the overhead light.

Decker heard himself cry out.

"Leave the fucking bears alone!" Angela shouted, and the trailer shook as the door slammed shut behind her.

They sat still in the dark for a moment.

"That's your wife?" Decker finally said to Chug.

"Till death do us part," Chug said, and he chuckled.

"She's crazy," Marlowe said. He got up and fumbled around lighting the kerosene lamp, then took another beer from the cooler. "She should be locked up."

"Never did like hunting, but she's gone overboard on this one," Chug said. He waved his thumbless hand. "Hell, man's a predator. Always has been and always will be. It's in his blood."

Bear had opened the door and was looking out into the darkness. "Total commitment," he said. "That's a woman who knows her enemy."

Chug shook his head. "Change of life. Knocks 'em clean out of the ballpark. Most women recover but sometimes they don't, and then look out."

"Maybe so," Bear said, but he turned and looked into the night again before closing the door.

"I guess the hunt's off," Decker said.

Marlowe stared at him. "You crazy?"

"I didn't come out here just to wimp out," Bear said. "I told you about that pâté, didn't I?" He closed his eyes and shivered. "Worth facing Angela Cramm for, I'll tell you that." Then he opened his eyes. "All the same," he said to Marlowe, "it's probably the better part of valor to wait till morning to go back down there."

Marlowe shrugged casually. "If it makes you feel better."

Chug winked at Decker.

In the morning the bait barrel lay on its side, empty, the cow head gone.

"God *damn*," Marlowe said.

Bear picked up a Ding-Dong wrapper that was taped to the rim of the barrel. Written in pencil on the inside of the wrapper was

LEAVE THE FUCKING BEARS ALONE

"Shit," Marlowe said. He swung away, stomping around on the hard-packed dirt, and then he suddenly raised his gun and fired into the sky.

"Jesus, Marlowe," Decker said.

"Jesus got nothing to do with it," Marlowe said. He closed his eyes and shouted, "Fucking shit!"

"Sometimes," Bear said softly, fondling the Ding-Dong wrapper, "the enemy outsmarts you. When you're at a disadvantage, you tend to get riled, and distracted, and then you're at his mercy. You got to know when to retreat."

"Sometimes you're full of shit, Bear," Marlowe said.

Bear patted the butt of his rifle. "It's something I learned in Nam," he said. "A worthy opponent deserves your respect." He turned toward the empty bait barrel and dropped to his knees. Laying his gun down in front of him, he placed his palms together in front of his chest and bowed from the waist three times; then he raised his hands up beside his head, his third fingers on his thumbs, and with his eyes closed he sang, "Ommmm."

Marlowe stood watching him. He leaned his gun against his hip as he pulled a pack of cigarettes from his shirt pocket, put one in his mouth, and lit it. Then he looked at Decker and drew a circle around his temple with the lighter.

Decker looked at Bear, singing on the ground beside the empty barrel, and felt himself relax for the first time since Marlowe's mother had burst into the trailer.

When he got home there was a message from Miriam on his machine. "It's Daddy," she said when he called her back.

"What's he up to now?" Decker said.

"He died last night," Miriam said, and she began to cry.

"Oh, God," Decker said. "Oh, honey, I'm sorry."

"He went in his sleep," she said. "He never woke up."

"Do you want me to come down?" Decker said.

"No," she said. "I'm not going to have a funeral."

"You know what that therapist said," Decker said. "Some kind of ceremony helps."

"Daddy would *hate* it," Miriam said.

They laughed.

"He wanted you to have some of his ashes," she said.

"He did?" Decker said.

"Half for you and half for me," she said. "You were the closest thing he had to a son."

"Oh, God," Decker said. "What would I do with his ashes?"

"Whatever you want," Miriam said. She began to cry again. "He was all I had left in the world."

"Oh, honey, that's not true," Decker said. "What about the new boyfriend?"

"He doesn't count," she said. "I'm talking about the past."

Decker cursed his heart for leaping. "You've still got me," he said.

"Decker," she said, "I've been meaning to tell you. I'm going to get married again."

He closed his eyes.

"Decker?" she said. "Oh, God, what a wrong time to tell you."

"It's okay," he said. "Myron already told me. Keep the ashes. I don't need them."

"It was one of his last requests," she said. "I'll send your share as soon as I get them back."

He hung up and opened his eyes, and he thought of all the people he hadn't spoken to in years. Most of them he had nothing to say to now. He didn't want to know about their lives, their families, or their plans for the future. And God knew he didn't want to reminisce.

"Well, what the hell *do* I want?" he said to Bad Cat, who sat watching him with perfectly round eyes. It was clear what Bad wanted, anyway. He opened a can of food and put it down, but Bad Cat looked away until Decker went into the other room; Decker heard the bells on his collar tinkle delicately as Bad Cat snuck up on the dish and inhaled his Fisherman's Feast.

When the winter rains began, they were not the abrupt cloudbursts that Decker knew from the Midwest but a deadening of the sky, and then a steady, endless deluge that went on for days, as if God had opened a faucet in heaven. The inches mounted up and the clay soil drank until it was saturated, and

then the depressions and hollows in the earth filled up and over-
flowed and the seasonal creeks began to trickle, and one day
later they were full and rushing along toward the rivers, carrying with them a year's supply of pine needles and oak leaves and
the ashes of the thousands of trees that had burned in August.

Decker stared out at the streaming woods and thought it
was a good idea to do stream surveying in the dry months. Fry
Creek was small but its high-water channel was twenty-five feet
wide, and it was not something he would like to stand in the
middle of once the winter rains began. He could imagine all the
effluvia, the branches and human waste and beaver dams that
would sweep downstream as the water built up. He hoped the
young couple with the marijuana plants had remembered to res-
cue their blue pots before the water rose.

He had just started making coffee when the sheriff's car
drove up into the yard, and Sheriff Floyd Peach got out and ran
through the rain up onto the porch. He opened the door as he
knocked, and walked over and sat down at the kitchen table,
leaving a trail of muddy footprints across the floor.

"Come on in," Decker said. "I just got up. Coffee?"

"Don't mind if I do," Floyd Peach said.

"It'll be a minute," Decker said, sitting down across from
him. "What's up, Sheriff?"

"Well," Floyd Peach said, leaning back in his chair and gazing at Decker from under half-lowered eyelids, "we been having
some unpleasantness up the road the last few days."

"Unpleasantness?" Decker said.

Floyd Peach nodded. "There's some folks live around here,

their families have been here a long time. You know, they came before there was anybody else; they had the woods to themselves for a long time and they don't like to change?"

Decker nodded.

"They're not what you'd call educated," Floyd Peach said, leaning forward. "But they are not your survivalists. They don't stockpile automatic weapons. They may be religious. Some singing, some Bible-thumping. But they aren't catastrophists."

"Yes?" Decker said, getting up to pour the coffee.

"I don't want to cast aspersions," Floyd Peach said. "Nor blame. Lord knows we're heading for showdown in this country, but I sure as hell don't want it to start here, not on my watch."

"I would guess not," Decker said. "Toast?"

"Don't mind if I do," Floyd Peach said. "Not to say we *don't* have survivalists around here. This is a Mecca for survivalists. There's all kinds of home schooling goes on in the hills. Tell you what, there are certain people around here I would not mess with if I wasn't the law."

The toast popped up and Decker handed a piece to Floyd Peach, who buttered it thoroughly.

"It's a question of rights," Floyd Peach said. "I am the last person to want to abridge any rights. But I'll tell you this." He pointed the toast at Decker and shook it severely several times, so that several little drops of margarine flew through the air and speckled Decker's glasses. "This country's overpopulated as it is, and getting worse. There are more illegal aliens in this county than there are police."

"Really?" Decker said.

"Believe it," Floyd said. "Here's what I'm getting at. Democracy is not necessarily compatible with massive overpopulation. Something"—he got up and dropped another piece of bread into the toaster—"has got to give. And *I* do not want it to be law and order."

"No," Decker said. "Put one in for me, too, will you?"

"Surely," Floyd Peach said. He walked over to the window. "Big garden. Have any luck with it?"

"Not what I'd expected," Decker said. "It was such a dry summer."

Floyd Peach nodded. "El Niño," he said. He walked back to the table and picked up his coffee cup. "It's here to stay. The weather is permanently changed. That's why all the darker races are coming north."

"Ah," Decker said. "Well." He got the toast from the toaster. "So what's this business up the road?"

"Nothing that should alarm you," Floyd said. "A little gunplay."

"Anybody get hurt?"

"Not to my knowledge," Floyd said. "Just some mushroom pickers exercising their First Amendment rights."

"Free speech?" Decker said.

Floyd looked at him a little scornfully. "Right to bear arms. You might want to stay out of the woods these days. You ever find that dog?"

"No," Decker said. "He never came back."

"Probably stolen," Floyd Peach said. "Drugs, guns, and dogs, in that order. After that it gets down to videocams and such." He shook his head. "The electronics market's so saturated I don't know what they do with them. Drugs and guns, now, have an infinitely large market."

"But dogs?" Decker said.

"Everyone loves dogs," Floyd Peach said. "Well, take it easy. You hear anything, stay inside and give us a call."

"Thanks for stopping in, Sheriff," Decker said.

"It's my job," Floyd Peach said.

Decker stood on the porch watching Floyd Peach drive slowly down the road through the light drizzle. The law was the law the world around, and violence was inherent in human nature, but at least in the city it was leavened by a little art, a little music, a wee bit of higher education. It was easy, in the city, despite the nightly news and the morning editions, to believe that enlightened people were in control. Here, though, he had begun to suspect that it just wasn't so. The genteel and educated of the world lived only micromillimeters away from a brutish, violent reality.

Bad Cat was creeping on his belly through the remains of the garden. Decker aimed his finger at him, following him carefully until Bad Cat stopped and crouched beneath the pyracantha. Then he shouted, "Pkew!" and jerked his hand, and like lightning Bad Cat pounced and caught a junco.

"Drop it!" Decker yelled. He ran down the steps and across the yard toward Bad Cat, who hunched into a commando crouch over his trophy. "Give it here," Decker said, grabbing Bad Cat by the neck and pulling him away.

It was too late. The bird looked untouched but it lay

motionless on the wet pine needles, its eyes closed and its silly beak tucked down into the soft feathers on its chest.

"You bad cat," Decker said sorrowfully. He let Bad Cat go and picked up the little bird, which weighed less than nothing.

At the foot of Decker's driveway an engine coughed and turned over, and Decker looked down to see Bear's truck back out of the thicket of young cedars. It turned and groaned up the gravel into his yard.

"Got yourself another dead bird?" Bear said, getting out of the cab and coming up to where Decker stood.

Decker showed him the little bird in his hand, and then knelt down in the mud beside the steps and dug out a hole and dropped it in. "Damn cat."

"Nature's way," Bear said.

"Floyd Peach was here before you," Decker said, leading the way back into the kitchen. "Investigating some shooting."

"Floyd Peach couldn't solve a crime if it bit him on the dick and hung on," Bear said. He grimaced at the footprints in the kitchen. "The man don't even wipe his feet."

"I imagine when you're the law you don't have to," Decker said. "What brings you around so bright and early?"

Bear handed him a soggy brown paper bag. "I been out since the crank of dawn," he said. "Matsutakes. Ever had one?"

"No," Decker said, looking into the bag at a dozen large flat mushrooms. "I've heard of them, though."

"A culinary orgasm," Bear said. "Plus they're paying seventy bucks a pound for them down in town."

"Holy cow," Decker said.

"Shit, that's nothing," Bear said, pouring himself some coffee and sitting down at the table. "In Japan they pay a thousand bucks for just one of these babies. One bite of this magic mushroom and a man can keep it up for a week."

"Wow," Decker said, taking a mushroom out of the bag and looking closely at it.

"Has to be the right one, though," Bear said. "Picked at the right moment, the right size and texture, properly prepared. Preferably sautéed lightly in sesame oil, with a drop of sweet ginger wine."

He leaned back and crossed his ankles, which were encased in heavy, muddy work boots. "This is a good year for them, after the fire. Except, you know those gook pigs everybody's got? People get tired of them and turn 'em loose in the woods, and now there's a bunch of them running wild, tearing up the forest floor and destroying the market. They been trained for centuries to find mushrooms in the ground. It was part of their religion."

"These pigs have a religion?" Decker said.

Bear leaned over and slapped him lightly on the stomach with the back of his hand. "You think it helps a man's performance, imagine what it does to a pig."

Decker stared out at the forest, where potbellied pigs and trigger-happy mushroom pickers crept through the undergrowth plundering the forest of its valuable fungi. "So were people shooting at you?" he said.

"Huh?" Bear opened his eyes. "Nah. They shoot right over your head, mostly. But it's BLM land. I know my rights."

"Do you shoot back?"

"Give 'em an inch and you know what they take."

"Yeah," Decker said. "I guess they do."

The UPS truck rumbled up into the yard and jerked to a stop, and the driver bounded up onto the porch. Decker opened the door.

"Hey there, Bobby," Bear said.

"Hey, Bear," Bobby said. He grinned at Decker and handed him a small gray box. "Early Christmas present."

"Not exactly," Decker said. The box was light, as if it were empty, but when he shook it a little it made a shifting sound, like sand. "My father-in-law's ashes."

"What is it with ashes?" Bobby said, lifting his hands in amazement. "That's the third one this week."

"Really it's only *half* his ashes," Decker said. "I'm splitting them with my ex-wife."

"Well, *that's* different," Bobby said. "What are you going to do with them?"

"I don't know," Decker said.

"Last guy had a Siberian pea shrub that needed a higher pH," Bobby said. He looked at his watch. "Well, miles to go before I sleep. Catch you later."

"Thanks," Decker said. He closed the door and stood holding the box in the middle of the kitchen.

Bear yawned and stood up. "To market to market." He looked closely at Decker. "You okay? You want me to stick around for a while?"

"No, I'm okay," Decker said.

"Tell you what," Bear said. "I got a project I could use your help on."

"Me?" Decker said.

"You," Bear said. "Can you take some time next week? It would involve some camping."

"In the rain?"

Bear shrugged. "Back of my truck is pretty dry."

"What's the project?"

Bear gazed out the window. "Something that might interest you," he said. "I can't really talk about it now."

"Not hunting," Decker said.

Bear shook his head. "Not hunting."

"Well," Decker said, "sure."

He held out the bag of matsutakes, but Bear held up his hand. "Those are for you. Don't worry, wrong time of season for those effects I was talking about. I wouldn't do that to a single man. Eat your fill."

"Thanks," Decker said. "Thanks for stopping by."

"No problemo," Bear said. "I'm just as glad to wait here till ol' Floyd's off the roads."

Decker watched him drive away, and then sat down and put the box of ashes on the table. He had expected to feel emotional at holding Myron's remains in his hands, but he felt next to nothing. He slit the tape and opened the box, and they looked like any ashes. They might have been the ashes he shoveled out of his stove every few days. He closed the box and put it in the cupboard next to the brown sugar.

. . .

Bear and Decker drove up into the mountains, along the banks of Fry Creek and past the turnoff that led to Chug's hunting camp, and as they gained elevation, the firs and pines shone black in the thin light. Overhead, hundreds of robins rampaged through the madrones, which were dripping with clusters of scarlet berries. Once a fox trotted across the road in front of them.

They drove a long way, higher and higher, and at every intersection Bear seemed to take the less-traveled road, so that in time they were bumping along a narrow track overgrown with blackberries and poison oak, and littered with scree and downed trees. As they crept along this section, they met the only other vehicle they'd seen on the whole trip; Bear had to back up until he reached a level area where he could pull off the road to let it pass. The driver lifted a finger from the wheel as the pickup rattled by.

"That was Sylvia Crane!" Decker said, twisting around to look.

"I couldn't say," Bear said.

When they finally stopped, Bear got a spotting scope out of the back and they walked up a weedy trail that narrowed until at last it was just a faint path through the dripping brush. It was dim in the woods but the clouds above the trees were bright, and in the top branches golden-crowned kinglets and chestnut-backed chickadees whistled endlessly. They walked for a half hour or so and then turned off the path. They had to bend low as they climbed uphill among the shiny red trunks of manzanitas.

"Quiet now," Bear said as they reached the top. "Keep down." On their knees they crawled to the crest of the hill and hunkered beside a boulder. In the distance a dozen mountain ridges marched off to the horizon, the valleys between them stuffed with fog.

Directly across from them, on the other side of a narrow canyon, was a grassy meadow that had burned years ago. Black snags and stumps rose here and there among the soggy seedheads of last summer's fireweed and thistle, and when Decker looked through the binoculars, he could see that baby cedars and pines had begun to grow in the shelter of the burned snags. He scanned the hillside as Bear set up the scope.

"There," Bear whispered, peering into it and pointing toward a scramble of blackberry canes on the far hill.

Decker looked but could see nothing.

"Try this," Bear said, scooting over to let him look through the scope.

Decker squinted into the eyepiece and twisted a knob, and out of the browns and reds and grays of the wet hillside a bear sprang into focus, ambling along the edge of the clearing. As it reached a clump of brambles it stopped, and Decker saw its grayish tongue wrap around a cluster of wizened berries and pull them into its mouth. It moved on, in no hurry. The bear's snout turned up just a bit, and it had a hump on its shoulders.

"Lila la Griz," he said.

The silver fur rippled in waves as she emerged from the shelter of the trees. She sat down and reached with a massive paw into a dark crevice between some rocks, and as she pulled her paw out and put it to her mouth, a cloud of moths flew up around her, fluttering white in the rain. She licked her fingers clean and reached in again.

"Fattening up for winter," Bear said, watching through the binoculars.

Lila ate several helpings of moths and then lumbered downhill, nosing among the rocks. She sat and ate again. Then she lay back, her forepaws dangling in the air above her chest, and wriggled around on some low-growing ceanothus. They could hear a deep, drawn-out groan of pleasure echoing down the hill.

"How did you know she was here?" Decker said.

"She's been under surveillance since she broke out," Bear said. "She's probably going to den up somewhere around here for the winter. Then in the spring we'll move her back to Montana."

"Trap her?"

"Nope," Bear said. "Persuasion. We're just going to keep her moving in the direction she wants to go."

"You can't really believe it will work," Decker said.

"Decker," Bear said, "the longest journey starts with a single step."

It was dark when they got back to the truck. Bear started the engine and turned on the heater full blast, and he rummaged around behind the seat. "Ready-to-eat," he said, pulling out a couple of cans. He opened them and the cab was full of the odor of canned meat. "In country guys were always complaining about the so-called food, but once I got out of there I dreamed of canned turkey and okra for years."

"Who all," Decker said, taking a can and poking at the contents with a plastic fork, "is involved in this?"

"Some things I can't tell you," Bear said.

"Angela Cramm?" Decker said.

"I'm naming no names," Bear said.

"That *was* Sylvia Crane, though," Decker said.

Bear nodded. "On her own time, though," he said. "No way Wildlife knows about this."

"Bear," Decker said, "why is this so hush-hush?"

Bear leaned his head back and looked at the ceiling, and the breeze from the heater fan ruffled the ends of his beard. "I've lived here a long time," he said. "I know the people around here. News got out that the griz was around, half the population of the valley would be up here with AK-47's."

"Why doesn't the Wildlife Department just tranquilize her? They could just fly her back to Montana."

Bear popped open a beer and took a drink. "They," he said, "are not us." He wiped his mouth with the back of his hand. "What we're doing ain't official policy."

"What about you?" Decker said. "A few weeks ago you wanted to shoot her yourself."

Bear chewed and swallowed for a while. "It was one of those times," he said at last, "when I saw the light. Something just clicked in me." He turned and looked seriously at Decker in the strange dim light of the overhead lamp. "There's more important things in life than having fun, Decker." He opened a can of peaches. "So you want to help out with this project?"

"Of course," Decker said. "But what can I do?"

"Just keep your eyes peeled," Bear said. "Nobody can get at her if we're here keeping an eye on her."

Bool sheet, Decker thought to himself, but aloud he said, "I can do that."

They slept in the back of the truck. There was so little sound in the nighttime woods that what noises there were zoomed in close: the dripping of leftover rain from the trees onto the bracken; an occasional rustling in the fallen leaves; and, louder and louder, the sound of rock music and children's voices and the distant ringing of a faraway telephone—Decker's tinnitus, which grew more annoying with every passing year.

"So," Bear said as they lay in the darkness, "what do you think you'll do with your father-in-law's ashes?"

"I don't know yet," Decker said.

"There's this one cult in Cambodia that just lays the whole body out in the jungle," Bear said. "They believe their spirits go into the animal that eats them. They spend their whole lives praying to be eaten by a white tiger."

"We spread my son's ashes at sea," Decker said.

"Ah, cremation," Bear said. "Going up in flames is appealing, in its way." He began to snore.

Decker thought of the way Sam's ashes had drifted on the surface of the dark water for a few moments before they began to sink out of sight. Then he thought about Lila la Griz, somewhere not so far away. He hoped she had a warm place to sleep. He liked the idea of watching over her. He lay picturing people stationed here and there in the woods, their eyes flicking around like Secret Service agents', their hands full of binoculars and cellular phones. He saw himself standing behind a fir tree, whispering into a megaphone, "There's no place like home"; and Lila, thinking she's caught something on the wind, lifting her head and moving her nose back and forth, back and forth, her nostrils wide and her small eyes straining to see something move—but the line of witnesses holds very still, not breathing.

"Montana," Decker whispers, and Lila heads east.

It was a pretty vision, and he tightened his eyes so hard against it that he woke up. He stared up at nothing in the dark and wished he could be optimistic about Lila's chances of getting home.

"Now Marlowe," Bear said, so suddenly that Decker jumped, "he wants his ashes packed into a shotgun shell and fired at a cougar." He turned over and his breath touched Decker's cheek as he spoke. "Chug's half buried already. They put his legs in the Odd Fellows cemetery."

Decker laughed. "What about his thumb?"

"It got mashed into particle board," Bear said. "Don't take it personal if I put my arms around you in the night."

"No," Decker said. "I won't."

Decker did his part. He took his turns sitting on the hillside watching Lila la Griz eat, while behind her the clouds flew past the peaks of the distant mountains and flocks of cedar waxwings and robins swept in great hordes through the treetops to feast on the madrone berries. After his shift he would be relieved by Bear, or by anonymous others who sounded their horns to let him know his watch was up and then hid their faces while he drove past them in the woods. They all watched in the drizzle until the drizzle one day turned to snow; and then after Lila la Griz tucked herself in for the winter in a space under a big rootwad on the side of the hill, they took turns sitting in the snow, making sure no one disturbed her. Every time Decker was there no one came within miles of her. He didn't know what he would have done if they had come, but they didn't.

The snow was not deep and the winter was not long, but spring was still a long way off when Lila woke up, hung around outside her rootwad for a few days, and disappeared. It was nobody's fault. One morning she just didn't show up, and she didn't show up again the next day. The watchers spread out in ever-widening circles around her empty den, searching for hide or hair, but there wasn't so much as a hint of spoor.

"I'm not surprised," Bear said. "How do you think they survive anyway? Not by standing around waiting to be counted."

Decker pictured a crowd of bored grizzly bears standing in a clearing in the woods while someone with a clipboard walked slowly by, counting each one. "Come on, come on," one of the bears said grumpily, "I haven't got all day."

"I hope she got away," he said. He thought of the miles and miles of empty space between Lila la Griz and Montana, and of the cold hard floor of somebody's single-wide.

"She's a wild animal," Bear said. "They've got powers we can't even imagine."

Spring was in the air. The snow was melting fast, running in streams down the slopes and across the roads, heading for the river. The spotted leaves of fawn lilies suddenly cluttered the forest floor, and one day their delicate orchid blooms appeared in the darkness of the woods. The hills that had been burned were carpeted with brilliant green seedlings, and even in gardens with ten-foot fences thin does with new fawns materialized to serenely devour the new growth on the roses.

"I'm putting you on golden eagles," Sylvia Crane said when Decker went into the Wildlife office to get his spring assignment. "We need to count nests and nestlings."

"Why?" Decker said.

Sylvia narrowed her eyes a little. "Baseline information," she said. "We have to be able to document their decline." She picked up a stack of contour maps and dropped them in his arms, and tucked a list of possible nesting sites under his chin. "What we want," she said, sitting down behind her desk and putting her feet up, "is evidence that these sites are in use this year." She smiled up at him. "I don't really expect you to find any. Golden eagles nest in snags, like ospreys, but a lot of the time they're in dense growth. We could probably see them from small planes but we haven't got sightseeing flights in our budget."

"I'll do my best," Decker said, heading for the door.

"Oh, and while you're up there," Sylvia said casually, "you might keep your eyes open for charismatic megafauna."

"Like grizzlies?" Decker said.

"I don't expect you to find any of those either," Sylvia said, "but you never know." She smiled again, and he smiled, too.

Leaving the freeway behind, Decker drove past a dozen damp-looking ranchettes, thin brown smoke rising from the chimneys and in the yards raggedy mules and llamas staring aimlessly into space. The road he was on turned into gravel, and the houses stopped and the trees closed in overhead, blocking out what there'd been of the sky. He turned onto another, thinner road, and drove up into the mountains.

At an unmarked intersection he stopped and unfolded the map Sylvia had given him. It showed a roadless area on the other side of a ravine, and in the middle of it was a red star that marked the place where someone had once reported seeing a nest.

Decker took the road to his right. It plunged him into a patch of huge trees, trees that were so big that he thought they might be a thousand years old. They towered above him, hung with trailing lichens and furry with moss, and ferns covered the forest floor at their feet. At the very edge of the road were bare ceanothus and currant, and even as he drove by he could see how thick the tips of their twigs were, how ready to burst into leaf and bloom. True spring would break out any day now.

He drove around one final eroding bend and the truck rolled down a suddenly well-graveled road into a big flat open space that was clearly a helicopter pad and staging area for giant logs. Some time ago, though. No indication that helicopters came here anymore. Right now what was here was a pickup truck, with Marlowe Cramm beside it with his earmuffs on and his high-heeled logger's boots caked with mud and his chainsaw screaming to beat any band in the world as he bucked up a huge Port Orford cedar.

Marlowe had heard nothing, of course, and Decker had to walk clear out and around into his field of vision to get his attention. When he did, Marlowe slowly reached to turn off the chainsaw, and he straightened up and took off his ear protection in very slow motion, and the pupils of his eyes slowly contracted as his brain came back in from space.

"Hey there," Decker said. "What's going on?"

Marlowe stared at him for a moment and then said, "Cutting wood."

"Ah," Decker said. "Ever see any golden eagles up here?"

Marlowe looked as if he thought Decker might be mad. "If there was any, I'd know it, but there ain't," he said.

Decker knew that, given the way animals live in the woods, an eagle could land in the clearing and walk up behind Marlowe and screech, and Marlowe, deep in his earmuffs with the chainsaw wailing, would never know. But he just said, "Well, it's a real old report. What brings you up this far?"

Marlowe, still holding the chainsaw poised to slice into the cedar on the ground, said, "Wood."

"Right," Decker said. He looked around. "This private land, or what?"

Marlowe gestured with the chainsaw, indicating nothing. "This part is," he said.

"Ah," Decker said. "Mind if I look around?"

"Free country," Marlowe said, "so far." He pulled the starter on the saw, but when it didn't start he took the opportunity to say, "You can get a good view from over there," and he nodded toward the end of the clearing where a pile of logs and brush stood twenty feet high.

"Thanks," Decker said, and he walked toward it. The

chainsaw caught as he climbed up onto the slashpile.

Marlowe had told the truth. Below him lay the whole river valley, the part that ran east and west beside the freeway. It was a lesson in the spread of humanity, Decker thought, the way the view showed so clearly the ever-expanding circles of towns, houses covering the valley floor before they infiltrated the hillsides, road after road after road flowing out of the little side valleys and into the long gray ribbon of highway that ran toward the coast. The whole scene looked man-made, the cunning little houses and barns, the manicured lawns and well-marked boundaries.

When he first moved here the woods had seemed like a vast unpeopled cushion of vegetation, a doughnut of healthy trees surrounding the occasional hole of human society—a person here, a person there, someone down the road who you could go and visit if you felt like it; and around everything a huge, nearly impenetrable barrier of forested mountains full of animals and birds and healthy trees. But Decker knew now that was some other planet, one of the ones screaming with emptiness in the heavens. Even in the deepest heart of the woods, Decker felt that if he closed his eyes for only a second, he would open them to find the subdivisions subdivided, trees falling by thousands, and everywhere culverts and asphalt and people breeding.

He climbed carefully back down the slashpile, stepping from branch to branch, quick visions of slipping or dislodging one of the larger logs tilting in and out of his brain. He walked back to his truck, lifting a hand as he passed Marlowe, who was paying full attention to the chainsaw in his arms and simply jerked his chin in response.

Decker drove back up to the top of the road, and when he rolled down the truck window, the chainsaw was still going. He stared at the map for a while and decided to go to one more place today, farther up the same valley. He had plenty of gas. He drove back to the intersection and this time turned south, and after a few miles the road went up again. Options started opening up and he chose carefully, always checking to see what looked like the most likely road to lead him high up and close to the "x" that marked the place where someone in some dark age thought they had seen a golden eagle nest.

He didn't know where these reports came from. Everyone, he supposed. Hunters and loggers and BLM biologists and inholders. Stewardesses peering out the cabin windows as planes swept low over the mountains. Balloonists from Kansas. Everybody wanted in on the eagle act.

The road narrowed, and the skeletons of last year's woolly mulleins, blackened by the winter rains, crowded close along the little-used tracks. He pulled the truck over to the side of the road and got out. After the sound of his engine, his ears throbbed with the silence. He stood still, scanning the distance, waiting for the sound waves whirling around his head to slow and stop. When they did he could hear the air whistling through the hairs in his nostrils, it was that quiet.

He scrutinized the hills on the far side of the gulch, hoping for the flat huge mass of sticks in the top of a snag that would be an eagle nest. Something at the edge of his field of view caught his eye and he moved his binoculars upward, scanning back and forth, until he found it: a black silhouette high over a naked ridge. It was a raptor, gliding above a distant meadow. Now and then as it turned in the sky, its tail caught the sun and gleamed for a brief second before the bird went black again.

Red-tailed hawk.

It was getting too dark to look for the golden eagle nest. "It's a day," Decker said, and he tucked the lens covers back on his binoculars, peed off the side of the cliff, and swung back into the truck. It was mid-afternoon, which now, two weeks away from spring, was as thin-lit as late evening would be in what he liked to consider the real part of the year, God's time, mid-summer. The sun was lazy this far north, lying low in the sky all day, breaststroking around a few inches above the horizon.

Once, Decker had thought his life would balloon out, billowing into the future, loaded with the hot air of possibility. Now, though, he had lost all the possibilities, one after another. He remembered himself as a child, doing the things that American children did, dancing with excitement at Christmas or Easter or summer vacation. Little did the little Decker know what lay in store. At what point would he have turned back? At what point would he have stopped?

For all that, why didn't he stop now?

He was like an ox. He lowered his head for the yoke and once it was on he just kept walking, pulling whatever the load was. It never occurred to him that he could do anything else. Whoever thought up the concept of free will certainly had been imaginative.

"My life is in the woods now," he said aloud as he drove. It was true, too. The only thing to come back to town for was to

feed Bad Cat and to pick up his meager paycheck from Wildlife.
Buy food. Go to the bank once in a while to get money, fill up the
gas tank, renew his library books. There was so little he needed.

He eased the truck over the washboard road in second gear,
and suddenly, just for a moment, the presence of Bob's ghost
beside him was overwhelming. Decker even looked quickly at
the passenger seat, cursing himself as he did. When had he
started seeing things out of the corners of his eyes? All his life?
Or just lately, just in the last few years when it seemed that
everyone in his life was slipping away, quick movements that
were gone before he could even look for them?

The truck rounded a sharp curve and there in the road was
a cougar. Decker had never seen a cougar before, but he knew
what it was. It stood in the middle of the road, gazing incuri-
ously right through the windshield into his eyes. He blinked
and it was gone. He flipped on his headlights and drove on home.

When he reached for a coffee filter the next morning,
Decker saw the box of ashes sitting beside the brown sugar. He
took it down and set it on the table. It was high time he did
something with poor old Myron. Supposing he made a mistake
some bleary morning and sprinkled Myron on his bran flakes?

A car door slammed and he looked out to see Floyd Peach
coming across the yard.

"You're big on early morning visits," Decker said, opening
the door.

"That's community policing," Floyd said. "We're always
there when you need us." He walked into the kitchen and headed

for the table. At a sudden sound behind him he yanked the gun out of his holster and spun around just as Bad Cat slipped out of the cupboard under the sink, letting the door bump closed behind him. He ignored Floyd Peach and stalked across the room to sit beside his empty dish and glare at Decker.

"You seem a little jumpy," Decker said.

"You never know," Floyd said. He put his gun away. "The fact is, we've had some reports of suspicious behavior up around here."

"More mushroom hunters?" Decker said. He opened a can of Mackerel Delight and the sharp smell of fish burst into the room.

Floyd Peach wrinkled his nose. "Could be, but the M.O. is different." He sat down at the table. "Thought you might be able to tell me something about it."

"Me?" Decker said.

Floyd Peach gazed at him. "There's a lot of woods up here," he said. "We discussed this back last fall, as I recall. Talked about the various lifestyles represented. How a man can do pretty much whatever he wants to do, as long as nobody else is hurt or inconvenienced and no laws of the land are blatantly disregarded."

He put his hands palms down on the table. "Now, I don't believe for one instant that you are the type that's what we call prone to crime. But you know what I have seen time and time again out here? That when you give a man enough rope, he will end up hanging somebody. And my job is to see that it's himself and himself only."

Decker stood holding the coffeepot. "Sheriff, are you saying you suspect me of committing some crime?"

Floyd smiled. "Now, don't go putting words in my mouth that I never said," he said. "I just dropped by, in a community sort of way, to have a talk, and to ask you a few questions."

Decker leaned against the counter beside Bad Cat, who was noiselessly eating mackerel. "Ask away."

Floyd reached into his shirt pocket and took out a piece of paper, which he unfolded. He took a pair of glasses from the other pocket and put them on. "Now," he said, "there have been several reports of an unidentified male Caucasian driving seemingly aimlessly around on the government roads. When questioned, said male claimed to be hunting for quote golden eagle nests unquote."

"That's me," Decker said.

"I'm glad you said that," Floyd Peach said, "because the license number that was reported matches the one on your Toyota pickup."

"Sheriff, that's my job," Decker said. "I'm working for the Wildlife Department."

Floyd Peach wrote something down on the piece of paper. "We'll check that out," he said. "Meanwhile, do you mind telling me why Wildlife would send you out looking for golden eagle nests in country where golden eagles have not been seen in this century?" He looked at Decker over the top of the glasses. "You sure you ain't been sent looking for wild geese?" And he laughed loudly.

"Are you accusing me of something, Sheriff?" Decker said. He felt like a fool saying it.

"No, no, no," Floyd said. He folded the paper up and put

it away. "You know, there's a lot of drug manufactury goes on around here. Pot, LSD, methamphetamine, crack cocaine, you name it. People get nervous. They don't want that kind of business disrupting their family values. And when they hear a phrase like 'golden eagle nest' seemingly totally out of context, why, naturally, they suspect that it could be some kind of code."

"Sheriff," Decker said, "a dozen eagle nests have been reported around here. This area is prime habitat for golden eagles. If you talk to Sylvia Crane at Wildlife, she'll explain everything."

"No doubt," Floyd Peach said. He took something else from his pocket and held it out toward Decker. "You recognize this woman?"

"That's Angela Cramm," Decker said.

"Uh-huh," Floyd said. "You know her socially, of course?"

"Well, no," Decker said, and to his fury he felt himself blushing. "No, I wouldn't say I know her. I've met her." He described their meeting beside Fry Creek, but he left out the part about their second meeting, later that night, in Chug Cramm's trailer.

Floyd Peach wrote some more things down on the folded paper, and then he looked up and said, "Angela Cramm is missing."

"Missing?" Decker said.

"She hasn't been seen since early winter," Floyd said. "Maybe not too long after you met her at"—he looked at the note he'd written—"Fry Creek."

"I thought she was sort of underground anyway," Decker said.

Floyd looked at him closely. "Funny choice of words, isn't it?"

"What?" Decker said. "No. I thought she was an eco-activist. I thought she liked her whereabouts to remain unknown."

"Well, you might have something there," Floyd said. He picked up the box of Myron's ashes and shook it. "Human remains, huh?"

"My father-in-law," Decker said.

"Just as a matter of routine," Floyd said, "I'd appreciate it if you'd let us get these analyzed. Just for the record."

"Sheriff," Decker said, "that's my *father-in-law's* ashes. My ex-wife sent them to me. You can ask her. You can ask the UPS guy. You can ask Bear Franklin, he was here when they got here."

"Well, we'll do all that," Floyd said. "Though just for your information, Bear Franklin ain't the most reliable witness around. He tends to suffer from post-traumatic stress disorder. You put him in an interrogation situation, he tends to go to pieces." He shook his head sadly. "If it's your father-in-law, as I'm sure it is, we'll get him back to you as soon as we can."

He stepped out onto the porch. "Another beautiful day. Spring is in the air." He turned to squint at Decker in the sharp gray light. "You know, I like you, so I'm going to give you a little bit of advice. I wouldn't get too tied up with the Wildlife Department. They're supported by tax money, and I'm going to tell you this." He shook Myron's ashes at Decker. "The taxpayers are a lit-tle tired of their hard-earned dollars going to support birds. Not to mention those damn owls."

He slapped the butt of his pistol. "'Nuff said! I'm on my way!" And he thumped down the steps and off to his truck.

. . .

After Floyd's visit the feeling of being watched settled over Decker like a shroud. When he stepped outside with the garbage, he felt as if someone had just ducked behind a tree at the end of the drive. As he walked across the yard to the compost pile, he felt as if he was doing it in a suspicious manner. The person behind the tree was probably whispering his movements into a tiny tape recorder concealed in a twig.

Decker dumped the garbage onto the pile and picked up the rusty shovel he kept there. He thrust it into the pile and then lifted it high off the ground and turned it over slowly, so that half-rotted grapefruit peels and moldering carrots could be easily identified as they fell to earth one by one.

"Compost," Decker said loudly. He had nothing to hide.

He could remember the feeling of being closed in, surrounded, in the city, but this was different. In the city he had been anonymous, but here everyone knew who he was. If they didn't, they had only to ask at the Family Mart, or to stop Floyd Peach as he was driving by and ask who drove that silver Toyota truck, wore that cherry-red Wildlife Department hat, and had a black-and-white cat that was so fat it couldn't get through its cat door anymore.

Maybe he should carry a gun, just to let people know that he wasn't easy pickings. It was an easy thing to sink into, this desire for a gun—it was a self-defensive move. Not even that. It was a pure statement, an announcement, nothing more than words, a sign: I KNOW THE RULES, carrying a gun would say. I BELONG.

Sheriff Floyd Peach would warn other people about him. "Ek-centric," Floyd Peach would say, squinting at some woman in her kitchen. "I ain't saying he's dangerous, I'm saying he's ek-centric and therefore unpredictable. You see him around, you give me a call."

When Decker walked into the Family Mart, the little chimes over the front door seemed very loud, and everyone— the clerk, a woman buying a lottery ticket, a teenaged girl carrying a huge toddler, and the toddler, too—all turned to look at him, and none of them smiled. The fake camera that was meant to deter thieves seemed to focus right on him as he walked past the cash register, and every time he entered a new aisle the stockboy just happened to be taking inventory down at the other end.

He loaded his basket with catfood and spaghetti sauce and a bottle of wine, and took it to the counter.

"This could be it," the clerk said as she started sliding his purchases across the scanner.

"Newman's Own?" Decker said.

"The quake in L.A.," she said. "Could be the beginning of the end."

"The end of the world, you mean?" Decker said.

"As we know it," she said. She stacked the catfood cans and drew them across the scanner in one fell swoop, causing a riot of little beeps. "It's not the quake, of course, it's the fires. The world will be consumed in fire."

"Ah," Decker said. "Is L.A. burning?"

"L.A. has been burning since 1968," she said, ringing up

the total. "Eleven ninety-four. We don't have to worry here, though. Paper or plastic?"

"Paper," Decker said. "Why not?"

"This valley's immune from fire, earthquake, and flood," she said as she placed the cans and jars in their preordained spots in the bag. "And at the last judgment a UFO's coming for us. A hundred and forty-four thousand of us will be taken away to another planet, where we will live in eternal glory."

She watched him pull bills out of his wallet. "Every time you pay in cash, it goes on your record."

"Yeah, I know about that one," Decker said. "Microchips, right?"

"Nope," she said, "that was primitive. Now the bills themselves are sensing devices that transmit directly to the information superhighway. What you buy, how much you spend, what size of bills you use—it all goes straight to the Oval Office." She ripped his receipt off the printer and handed it to him. "Six cents your change."

Decker grinned at the coins, just in case they were sensing devices, too. The folks in the Oval Office could check out his teeth.

"Daddy in custody!" Miriam said. "Being held as evidence!" And she was lost in laughter.

"Miriam, it's not funny," Decker said, laughing too. "I could be arrested. Everything I said came out wrong."

"Guilt is the human condition," Miriam said. "Maybe you'll be allowed to pay for your sins."

"I don't think that's the answer," he said. "So how's married life?" Saying it made him stop laughing at once.

"I wish things were different," she said. "I can't even say I think you'd like him, because I don't think you would."

"Surely that's irrelevant," Decker said.

"Yes and no," Miriam said. "Decker, I miss Daddy more than I ever thought I would."

"Strangely enough," Decker said, "so do I."

"What about you, Decker? What do you do with your time?"

I'm sinking farther and farther into a black hole, he thought. I spend my time as soon as I get it. "Well, I started a new project for Wildlife," he said. "I'm searching for golden eagle nests."

"Really?" she said. "Why?"

"I don't know," he said. "Because they're there. Or at least because my boss hopes they are."

"No, I mean why do you work for minimum wage?"

"I like the work," he said. "Miriam. How are you doing, really?"

She sighed. "I sort of live in a twelve-step program. One day at a time."

"Me too," Decker said.

"Oh, Decker," Miriam said, "I wish I could do something for you. I hope we can stay friends."

"We're friends," he said. "I think we really are."

He looked across the room at Bad Cat, who was lying on his back in front of the woodstove, his front paws in the air under his chin, his eyes closed into straight contented lines.

What was a friend anyway? At their very first tragedy he and Miriam had drifted apart, and now she had replaced him with a man Decker wouldn't even like, whose name he didn't even know. Bad Cat would probably do the same for a can of mackerel.

"*Risotto con funghi*," Bear said, waving the knife in greeting as Decker walked in.

"Bless you," Decker said. He handed Velveeta the wine as she kissed his cheek.

"A food fit for the gods," Bear said. "A northern I-talian dish. It needs careful cooking and totally fresh ingredients. I picked this"—he picked up a gray flat fungus from the cutting board—"ten minutes ago."

"Well, I'll trust you," Decker said. He sat down at the table and told them about Floyd Peach's visit.

"I can't believe he took your father-in-law," Velveeta said. "I can't see that there's any reason behind that."

"Floyd Peach don't need a reason," Bear said as he sliced an onion. "He's a turkey."

"I feel like I'm being watched," Decker said. "I step out my door and I think someone's behind a tree."

"Change is stressful," Velveeta said. "I think you represent change, Decker. People around here don't know how to handle it."

"Why do they have to expect the worst?" he said.

"Hell, you *are* the worst," Bear said. "Any logger worth his salt knows he's gonna lose his job if you find any birdie nests up in there. The environmentalists'll close off the woods."

"Nonsense," Decker said. "Well, only in nesting season."

"Hah," Bear said. "It's happened to 'em before." He turned on a burner and set a pan on it. "If you don't get a pan good and hot for onions, they just kind of sweat."

"I'm walking around under a cloud of suspicion," Decker said glumly.

"Most people around here live under a cloud of suspicion anyway," Bear said. "Makes you one of us." He lifted his glass in a toast.

"Maybe you could think of it as a cloud of possibility," Velveeta said. "A chance to enhance understanding between two different groups of people, Decker. Sort of like a cloud of belonging."

Decker shook his head. "Not exactly what I had in mind," he said. "Being suspected of drug dealing and murder."

He refilled their glasses and told them about the cougar he'd seen in the road.

"That's a kind of blessing," Velveeta said. "Cougars won't be seen unless they want you to see them."

"More news from beyond?" Decker said, but he felt with surprise that he said it with less sarcasm than usual. He felt with surprise that he sort of agreed with her.

"It may not be," Velveeta said, looking at him over the rim of her glass, "a *thing* they're trying to tell you. It may be just themselves—the essence of themselves—that they're trying to convey."

"Communication on a whole 'nother level," Bear said.

"Part of the great cosmic conversation," Decker said. He envisioned great swirling clouds of cosmic dust and sparkling planets whirling through space, trailed by songs strangely similar to those of humpback whales. Oh, what to believe?

"Them big cats breathe secrecy," Bear said. "They're there, and then they're not. Turn around and you see 'em, blink and they're gone. Just like happened to you."

"I was in the presence of magic," Decker said lightly, but Bear and Velveeta didn't laugh. He got up and strolled over to the window. The sill was cluttered with little baskets made from grapevines, each one holding a HELP! TURN ME OVER! rock. He took one of the rocks out of its nest and turned it over. On the bottom it said,

SUCKER!

"Sucker?" he said, amazed.

Velveeta smiled. "Every now and then you find one of those," she said. "Don't take it personally."

Decker shook his head. He stood turning the rock over and over in his hand, and looked out at the side yard. A Nubian goat was drinking from a bathtub under a large Douglas fir, and some chickens were scratching around in the mud, their stupid beady eyes intent on what they were doing. Piles of things—old barbed wire, a rusted reel lawn mower, a Flexible Flyer sled—were everywhere, last year's star thistle sticking up through them. Bear and Velveeta seemed to save everything they had ever owned.

At the sound of vicious crackling Decker turned around to see smoke rising from the pan where Bear had just dropped a chunk of butter.

"A little hot," Bear said. He took the pan off the burner and held it up in the air, away from the stove. "A few drops of oil will cool it off." With a flourish he picked up a bottle of olive oil and poured some into the pan, and it burst into flame.

"Look out!" Decker shouted. Without thinking he ran across the room and emptied his glass into the pan, and the wine exploded with a whoosh. Bear screamed as the flames shot up into his face. There was a sizzle of frying hair and a great cloud of smoke and steam billowed up into the room.

"Drop the pan, drop the pan!" Decker shouted, but Bear just stood there, hanging on to the burning pan, until Velveeta appeared in the middle of the smoke and poured a boxful of baking soda on the flames. With a slurping sound the fire sank down and was gone.

"Jesus," Decker said, waving the smoke out of his eyes. "Bear, are you all right?"

He peered through the smoke at Bear, who stood blinking at the blackened, smoking pan. His cheeks were flushed a bright red, and every hair on his face—his eyebrows, his lashes, and his huge full beard—had crinkled right up into a tight, crispy little curl.

"Oh, my God," Decker said. He stood clutching his empty glass. "I'm so sorry. God, how stupid. Are you all right?"

"Close your eyes, baby," Velveeta said. Bear obediently closed his eyes and she began to smear his face with the viscous moisture she'd squeezed from a spike of her huge aloe plant. "Decker, honey, oil and water don't mix. Didn't your mama ever teach you that?"

To Decker's embarrassment tears welled up and spilled

down his cheeks. "I guess not," he said. "I mean, I knew that would happen. I didn't think." He looked at Velveeta's long fingers gently sliding across Bear's red face, which glistened now with aloe juice. "Bear, I could have killed you."

"You always kill the thing you love," Bear said.

"Oh, honey, I don't think that's true," Velveeta said, standing back to look at his face.

"It's a poem," Decker said, sniffing stupidly.

Bear smiled, his eyes still closed. "We love the thing we kill, maybe. That's something I learned a long time ago."

"Death is part of life," Velveeta said, and she went back to smoothing juice onto Bear's brow.

Bear opened his eyes and looked at Decker. "Anywhere, man. Anywhere, any time. I told you it didn't have to be Nam." He shook his head, as if to clear his brain, and some charred hairs flew off. "What a rush."

Decker was halfway home when flashing blue lights appeared in his rearview mirror. "Oh, fucking shit," he said aloud, glancing at his speedometer as he slowed down to pull over. "Just what I fucking need." He rolled down his window and a fine mist blew into his face. Sheriff Floyd Peach walked up.

"Evening," Floyd Peach said. "Hurrying home?"

"Come on, Floyd, I wasn't speeding," Decker said.

Floyd Peach stepped back, lifting his hands. "Nobody said you were, son, nobody said you were." He came forward again and handed Decker the box he was carrying. "Saw your truck and thought I'd save myself a trip tomorrow. I got your father-in-law right here."

"Oh," Decker said. "Thanks. He passed the test?"

"Routine procedure," Floyd said. "What you going to do with them?"

"The ashes?" Decker said. "I don't know."

Floyd Peach folded his arms and looked down the road ahead of them into the darkness. "Tell you something," he said. "Don't keep 'em around too long. My wife put her mother in a box up in the garage, and it accidentally got took out to the landfill." He shrugged. "I didn't see what difference it made, but it still comes up when we have heated discussions." He leaned close. "As if it was *my* fault."

"Imagine," Decker said.

"Speaking of which," Floyd said, "my beddy-bye time. You drive careful, now."

"Good night," Decker said. "Thanks, Sheriff."

"Saved me a trip," Floyd said.

At home Decker opened a can of Cap'n's Choice and dropped it onto Bad Cat's plate. Bad stared at it in horror, then turned his back and sat down to clean his paws.

Decker sighed. "You are not an easy companion animal," he said to the back of Bad. "Now Bob, he appreciated every scrap I gave him."

Bad Cat stopped in mid-lick, staring straight ahead with his paw in the air. Then, relenting, he turned around and crouched over the plate of Cap'n's Choice and began to eat it with relish.

"Good Bad Cat," Decker said.

• • •

In the morning Decker took Myron down to the seasonal creek. After a winter of rain the trickle of water had swollen and popped its banks and now roared through the woods carrying leaves and hunks of lichen and a few small sticks. Myron might as well go along, Decker thought. Better than ending up in the landfill.

"So long, Myron," he said, and he held the box upside down over the stream and watched the ashes and the little chips of bone drop into the water. They sat there in a clump for a moment, until an oak leaf rammed into them. The clump began to erode, and ash after ash sank, or drifted, or simply dissolved into the rushing water.

He thought of the journey ahead of them—a long, cold trip, down through Decker's property and past the Family Mart and into town, where they would plunge through a culvert under the highway and pour out into the river. They would get separated from one another there and mix with the rest of the river water, and be carried along with fish and silt and illicitly dumped toxic substances, down to the mouth of the river and out to sea.

And there Myron's ashes would mingle with Sam's.

Decker wiped his eyes and smiled at the thought. A piece of comfort, where he had never thought to find it.

He turned and walked along the stream, looking for the rooster's grave. It wasn't there. He didn't know what he'd expected to see—yellow toes poking up out of the ground, perhaps. But he couldn't find anything—no disturbance of the ground, no log covering the spot, no gaping hole where the log had been rolled away. It was as if the rooster had never been.

He spent the day pulling up last year's slimy cornstalks and tomato plants and turning over the dirt in his garden. Even in the chilly air he worked up a sweat that didn't evaporate in the dampness, and after an hour he was soaking wet, his hair plastered to his head and his shirt pounds heavier than it had been starting out. Mid-afternoon as he stood catching his breath the sun broke through the clouds, and the shards of light refracting through the mist made him involuntarily squeeze his eyes shut and stumble blindly into the shade of the house.

He heard a tinny wheezing, and he squinted through the brightness into the woods behind the garden. High in the top of a Douglas fir he saw a fluttering flock of small birds. He got his binoculars from the kitchen and climbed up the bank, walking through the wet brush toward the tree. Twigs snapped and wet leaves swished under his feet but the birds paid no attention. Just another hominid in the forest. He stood still and put the glasses up to his eyes.

They were pine siskins, bright with their new spring plumage, and there were dozens of them, maybe a hundred, tseeing and flitting around. He could see insects puff up now and then from the treetop in a little smudge. What the hell kind of bugs hung around in the trees in late February? He wished the siskins would hold still. The pleasure of watching birds was that he was meaningless in their world, but that was the pain, too. He would have liked them to watch him back.

The sharp crack of a gunshot blew through the forest. Decker could feel it vibrate in his chest. Silence hit the siskin flock, and in one seamless motion they rose up and swept away over the tops of the trees. There were so many birds and the woods had gone so silent that he could hear their tiny wings beating the air.

He had just finished supper when there was a knock on the door and Bear stepped inside. His skin, though flushed and shiny, was unscarred from the flames, but his eyebrows looked as if they had been shaved off. His beard *had* been.

"My God," Decker said. "You look about twelve years old, Bear."

"This chin hasn't seen the light of day for twenty years," Bear said, rubbing it.

"I feel terrible about last night," Decker said.

"Forget it," Bear said. "Water under the dam. Lookit, I want to show you something I got in the mail." He took a photograph out of an envelope and handed it to Decker.

It was an overexposed Polaroid shot of sharp boulders and grim leafless shrubs poking up through patchy snow. On the back someone had written in pencil

ALMOST HOME!

"What's this supposed to be?" Decker said.

"Look there," Bear said, pointing. "In the upper right hand corner."

Decker peered at it. The brownish speck in the corner was too small to be identifiable, but he suddenly knew what it was. "Lila la Griz," he said.

Bear grinned and showed him the envelope. "Mailed in Bozeman, Montana," he said. "I expect Angela Cramm will turn up one of these days."

Decker felt his own face slide into a helpless grin. "I'll be damned," he said.

A car came roaring up the driveway, the horn blaring. When Decker opened the door the headlights hit him full in the face and then swept across the porch, and a Ford van decorated with painted flames slid to a stop, its front bumper a foot from the back of Bear's truck. The driver's door burst open and Marlowe Cramm jumped out in a crash of earsplitting music and stood before them waving his arms, dancing.

"Party time!" he shouted.

"Boogie on down!" Bear shouted.

Decker and Bear stood on the porch watching as Marlowe, still dancing, slid open the van's side door and took three beers from a cooler. He tossed two up to them and upended the third and chugged it; thin streams of beer ran out the corners of his mouth and into his beard, gleaming in the glare of the head-lights. The music stopped and the voice of the deejay blared out of the speakers.

Marlowe dropped his empty can into the cooler and took out a full one, and leaned back against the van. "Any luck with them eagles?" he said.

"Not yet," Decker said.

Marlowe cupped his hand behind his ear.

"Not yet," Decker shouted. "But I'm sort of getting into it. I really want to find one."

"I know what you mean," Bear shouted. "It takes on a meaning of its own. Like a vision quest."

The voice on the radio stopped, and for a moment all was silent. Suddenly abrupt, familiar bass notes pounded out of the speakers and shook the wooden porch beneath Decker's feet.

"'Louie Louie'!" Bear shouted. "All right!" He jumped off the porch and started to dance with Marlowe in the yard.

"Louie Lou-EYE!" they sang, and their heavy voices boomed out with the music and drove deep into Decker's chest, where something tore loose and was swept out into the night. He stood alone on the porch watching the men dance and thought of the great lost bear blindly making her way across the frozen snow. When he tipped his head back to take a drink of beer he thought for a second he saw the black shape of an eagle circling endlessly above him, silhouetted against the faint stars that were beginning to show above the line of trees, and he remembered the meteor shower over the burning hills.

"Oh-ohh, baby," Decker sang, and Bear reached up and grabbed his hand, pulling him down into the yard.

Bear's hand was cold and sharp with calluses. Yet under the skin Decker felt fragile finger bones and stony knuckles, buried in protective fat so soft it might have been left from Bear's long-gone infancy. He could feel the blood pulse through the arteries and out to the tips of the fingers and then, blue, back toward the heart. In another life he would have lifted such a hand to his lips, but in this one he danced and sang, and kept his eyes on the perfect light of the dripping sky.